My Stupid, Sad, Pathetic Life

VICTOR GASIOREK

Copyright © 2021 by Victor Gasiorek.

All rights reserved. No part of this book may be reproduced in any form or by any electronic or mechanical means, including information storage and retrieval systems, without permission in writing from the publisher, except by reviewers, who may quote brief passages in a review.

This publication contains the opinions and ideas of its author. It is intended to provide helpful and informative material on the subjects addressed in the publication. The author and publisher specifically disclaim all responsibility for any liability, loss, or risk, personal or otherwise, which is incurred as a consequence, directly or indirectly, of the use and application of any of the contents of this book.

WRITERS REPUBLIC L.L.C.
515 Summit Ave. Unit R1
Union City, NJ 07087, USA

Website: *www.writersrepublic.com*
Hotline: *1-877-656-6838*
Email: *info@writersrepublic.com*

Ordering Information:
Quantity sales. Special discounts are available on quantity purchases by corporations, associations, and others. For details, contact the publisher at the address above.

Library of Congress Control Number:	IN-PROCESS
ISBN-13: 978-1-63728-333-2	[Paperback Edition]
978-1-63728-334-9	[Digital Edition]

Rev. date: 05/13/2021

This novel is dedicated to both my incredible mother, Eva, and my father, Gregory, who passed way before their time. I miss them more than words can possibly describe, and I know that all they would've wanted was to see me and the rest of my family members living happy, successful, and loved lives. Rest in peace to my wonderful parents, who I miss dearly and will always miss for the rest of my life.

Chapter

The blood was all over my hands, arms, and even my face. The brand-new white T-shirt my mom had bought for me was soaked in the dark-red puddle of blood that was occupying most of the basement floor. I remember walking down those creaky old basement stairs to an extremely pungent stench and a bad feeling in my stomach. At first, I was simply frozen in fear. However, that turned into a panic that I had never experienced before, a fear and a reality that I would have to face for the rest of my life. I looked at the ten-gauge shotgun covered in blood on the floor to slowly panning up and saw my dad sitting in his old office chair with half of his head and face blown off. I approached the rotting corpse of who I thought was going to be my male role model for life: my father. As I walked closer, my heart started beating faster and it was getting harder to breathe. Plus my hands were so shaky you would've thought that I had Parkinson's disease.

"Daddy?" I asked. "Daddy, are you okay?!"

My daddy leaned forward and whispered my name. "Vincent."

I immediately woke up drenched in sweat and breathing very heavily. Another night, another nightmare of my past. As usual, I woke up to the sound of the couple who live on the top floor of my duplex fucking. I thought that maybe by now I'd be used to it, but no. The sounds of the woman screaming while being beaten in the late hours of the night to the sound of her achieving orgasm at least multiple times during the later hours of the morning has, without a doubt, not helped the fact that I've suffered from insomnia since I lost my father to suicide.

I will never forget the day that changed my life forever. I had just turned seven years old. About three weeks after my birthday, I awoke from a heavenly slumber. I got out of bed and did what I usually did: looked out the window to see if my parent's cars were in the driveway. If they were, that meant they were home and I'd get a delicious breakfast. If they weren't, that meant they were usually at work or out running some errands.

Anywho, I noticed that my mom's car was gone but my father's wasn't. What freaked me out the most was that I looked at the kiddy calendar my dad had bought me and saw it was Monday. Why wasn't Daddy at work but Mommy was? Time to investigate! I went downstairs, convinced that I was either going to find my father passed out on the couch after a night of drinking too much or out in the sunroom chain-smoking his favorite brand of cigarettes: Camel Blues. To my surprise, my father was nowhere to be found. I became very anxious and yelled, "Daddy?!" a whole bunch of times but heard nothing but the sound of silence. I then realized the basement was the only placed I hadn't checked; and boy, to this day I think it would've been better, or at least healthier, that I had not gone down there. But I did. Finding your father with practically his whole entire face blown off and his brains, teeth, and blood all over ceiling and walls is not something any kid should have to witness. But life's a bitch and then you die according to Nas and AZ.

    I got out of bed after lying there for about half an hour and thinking of how much better my life would be if my mom and dad were still here. Not even thirty years old yet, and both of my parents are gone like the wind. I put on the same shirt and pants that I've been wearing since last week and went to rock a wicked piss and brush my teeth. The couple upstairs finally stopped fucking, and I heard them get into an argument over whether a condom was used or not during their Monday morning sex session. I heard the alpha male of a boyfriend yell at his girlfriend before walking down the stairs of the duplex and slamming the door shut as if he had to prove a point by how hard he was by slamming the door. I obviously felt a little bit bad for the woman living upstairs, but at the same time, I didn't really give a fuck considering that I hardly give a fuck about myself and my own existence. I have lived inside of this crappy duplex for the last two years, and it by all means has not gotten better in any way whatsoever. Lola is the name of the sexually abused woman who lives on the top floor above me. She's very beautiful but very damaged at the same time. I have no problem or anything against damaged people because all I have to do is look at both of my wrists to remind myself that I am very damaged myself.

    I quickly ate a bowl of cereal with two pieces of toast. One piece smothered with hummus and sandwich meat and the other with peanut butter and jam. Afterward, I went outside to light up a cigarette, and at the exact moment that my flame went up, Lola opened her front door and sat on her steps to light up a cigarette. I pretended I didn't see her coming outside to smoke and just looked at my iPod Touch as if I had received a message or email from someone important. I didn't really want to talk to her. Judging by the sounds I heard from her last night and this morning, I assumed that she didn't really want to talk either, considering the same circumstances. So I sat there smoking my cigarette and realized that I had to go get my dose of methadone at the dope clinic. I walked up to the street and tossed my cigarette on the road. When I turned around, I noticed that Lola was staring at me while smoking her cigarette. She noticed the eye contact we had made and immediately looked away as if she had looked at me and into my eyes accidently.

I walked back inside of my duplex pretending that I had not even noticed Lola sitting there, never mind staring at me while I tossed my cigarette away. I decided to pack up my backpack to bring with me on my way to the methadone clinic. I felt really hungover from last night. Six Jack and colas, two cannabis sativa joints, and three or four 5mg Valium tablets. I didn't have a headache, and I wasn't nauseous or anything, I just felt a little depressed physically, mentally, and emotionally. The same way I feel most days except with a little more physical pressure on my chest, making it harder to breathe. I left my place and went on a ride to the dope clinic that I go to three times a week: Monday, Wednesday, and Fridays.

It was a very windy day, and almost all of the leaves were off the trees as fall had begun. Most people were wearing light jackets and parkas at this time as they walked up and down the sidewalks and main streets of the city. I took my skateboard because I was starting to feel a little bit sick and figured I'd get there faster on my board. There were quite a few people in the clinic, and I could tell that they were short on staff considering the size of the line inside. I waited for a good ten minutes at least before finally receiving my dose of methadone. I left the clinic feeling quite a bit better and decided to go to the convenience store across the street to get some more cigarettes. I smoked my last one on the way there; and for some reason, the smell of the tobacco, nicotine, and the hundreds of cancer-causing chemicals made me think of my father. I would always come from school and give him a big hug, and every single time his shirt smelled like cigarettes. No matter if it was a work shirt or a T-shirt, pants or shorts, he always reeked like cigarette smoke. His breath always smelled like either beer or Jack Daniels.

My whole family had problems with alcoholism. My mom and dad were both drunks, and my older sister was driving drunk one night on the way home from a party when she swerved off the road and drove directly into a tree. She died immediately on impact. This sent my mother into a type of alcoholic psychosis. She was never the same after that, and neither was I. My sister was six years older than me, and she had just turned eighteen and had all of her courses figured out for university. She wanted to become a drug counselor and then eventually become a psychiatrist afterward. Just like that, twelve years old and both my daddy and older sister were already six feet deep in the ground. My mom stopped believing in God and religion in general. I did the exact opposite. I became more religious and started praying more than ever, convinced that my dad and sister were looking down on me from the heavens above.

About eight years after my sister passed and I was twenty years of age, I started drinking very heavily myself. I was working at Burger King, and I literally had to bring a bottle of alcohol to work with me every day so I wouldn't go into alcohol withdrawal and start shaking uncontrollably. It was hell. I didn't remember anything from any of the shifts that I had worked. I would have to go into the bathroom and take a couple shots before going back to taking orders for customers. Some days I would buy myself fifty-dollar bags of cocaine just so I wasn't too blackout drunk at work and so that I could focus better and be somewhat coherent at work. My manager never really said anything, but I knew that she was on to me big time since my breath always reeked of vodka or whisky. I was a pretty hard worker, so she didn't really bring it up or mention anything about it—until I got caught, of course. I was in the staff bathroom, and I had chopped up two fat lines of blow and had my bottle of vodka on the bathroom sink. I had forgotten to lock the bathroom door, and out of everyone who worked there and everyone who could've come into the washroom, it was my boss who came in. I was doing a line as she walked in, and she froze at the sight of the line of coke on the bathroom sink and the almost half full bottle of vodka. She told me to immediately change outfits, give her back the employee uniform I had, and get out of the restaurant in ten minutes or else she was going to call the cops and tell them I had a schedule 1 narcotic on me.

That was about six years ago, and that was the last job I ever had. I have a DUI on my criminal record as well as possession of an illegal/controlled substance (LSD). I pled guilty to both charges, and because I had done exactly that, I never went to jail or prison. I just had to a shitload of community service and probation for two years. I finished all my probation hours and paid off every court fine that I had to my name about four years ago. My probation period ended around that time as well when I was twenty-two years old. I haven't been able to find employment since I was charged with my DUI and possession of acid.

I was driving home early in the morning, around 7:00–8:00 a.m., and I was coming down off a night full of crystal meth and paranoia. I just wanted to drive/get home as fast as possible so I could smoke some weed, pop some Valium, and go to sleep. I took a couple of real/non-pressed 2mg Xanax bars before I went behind the wheel and started driving home. I ended up falling asleep behind the wheel and woke up upside down in my car in the middle of the street. I had hit two parked cars, a fire hydrant, and, thankfully, no buildings/restaurants or human beings. I remember waking up and crawling out of my car window, and there was a circle of at least sixty to seventy people surrounding my totalled, upside-down, brand-new Honda Civic that I was leasing from a Honda dealership. The police ended up finding a quarter sheet of LSD and a couple bars of 2mg Xanax and a prescription I had for Tylenol 3. I admitted guilty before the officer even asked if I was fucked up or had anything illegal on me. I gave the police my mom's phone number, and after getting a ride in an ambulance to the hospital, I saw my mom waiting outside of the emergency response center chain-smoking while walking back and forth the way she always did when she was anxious or paranoid about something. She then saw me being pushed into the hospital on a stretcher and immediately ran up to me, claiming that she was my mom and wanting to be with her son. I told her exactly what had happened, and she wasn't too happy nor angry at the same time; she was just happy that I was alive. I remember my sister's lawyer coming into the room I was in and telling the officers who kept interrogating me to fuck off unless they wanted big legal trouble in court. And just like that, they left. I remember feeling completely numb toward everything while my mom and sister's lawyer were talking to each other. Everything became still, and even though they were both very close to me, I couldn't hear or make out what they were saying. Even the clock had stopped ticking. My heart was beating very fast, and I felt like absolute garbage from the previous night. My lung was in so much pain, and it was at that moment when I realized that it might've collapsed during my kickflip car accident that made local news. This was about the eighth or ninth time that my left lung was collapsed. The doctors then came back with my lung x-ray, and it revealed that it had definitely collapsed again. They hooked me up to IV hydromorphone and gave me a dose of 1mg lorazepam. I remember feeling the rush of the powerful opiate as the nurse injected me with it. Pins and needles covered my whole body, and the pain from my lung was gone just like that. Not only that, but I felt higher than a motherfucker. The first time I was exposed to opiates was when I was fifteen and in grade 10 when I collapsed my lung for the first time. I was given an IV shot of morphine, and let's just say, I never forgot that day and the feeling the IV opium had provided me with. I didn't like it because it made me very hot/sweaty and really nauseas. Eight collapsed lungs and five years later, I was once again in the hospital being loaded up with opiates and benzos. I was worried that I might go into alcohol withdrawal, but the nurses gave me a dose of lorazepam in the afternoon and another 1mg at bedtime.

    That was the last time that I had a collapsed lung, and I really hope it never happens again because it's extremely painful and lung surgery isn't the greatest procedure that anyone should have to go through. My mom always told me that it was because of my first collapsed lung and first-time exposure was the reason why I ended up turning into a heroin needle junky. I mean, it definitely makes sense, but for some reason I always disagreed with her.

    Since I was charged with DUI and my drug charge, I've had no choice but to go on welfare. No job will hire me even with the amazing resume that I had built for myself over the years.

    I finally skated home after buying myself a new pack of Camel Blues and decided to light one up before going inside. After smoking, I went inside and went on my laptop to entertain myself by searching the deep web and the dark web. One of my old friends had showed me how to access the dark web and how to protect your laptop or computer from being traced or drenched with spyware, malware, and viruses. I usually go on the dark web just to browse and possibly buy some drugs. I've bought heroin, Xanax, cocaine, and even DMT off the dark web before. I didn't really feel like getting drunk again, so I texted one of my friends who I usually buy heroin from, and he said he could help me find some as long as I shared a little bit with him. I agreed, of course, and met up with my friend later that night. He had bought the H and already cooked it and put it inside of needles so I didn't have to do it myself. So when I got home, I prepared myself for blastoff. I sat on my bed and tied a belt around my arm, thinking, *Time for a hug from God.*

Chapter

2

I was nearly drooling about the fact that I was about to get smacked with a nice strong shot of horse. The combination of that, some sativa dominant white widow, and the yellow 5mg Valiums my doctor prescribed me for anxiety and insomnia would send me into a deep black slumber of a sleep. Not to be disturbed by the gunshots down the street, the police sirens on Main Street, and Lola being beaten to a pulp by her boyfriend upstairs. I've never had the courage to ask Lola why her relationship with her boyfriend was so black-and-white and so violent. It bugged the shit out of me that she had never called the cops on him before, and I know this because I've lived under them for the last two years. I feel so bad for her, and Lord only knows where her boyfriend goes or what he does all day long before coming home and beating the shit out of poor, helpless Lola.

The H rushed through my veins, and I felt like I was starting to levitate off my couch and high toward the ceiling above me. I leaned back on my couch and put my feet up on my footrest and took a couple of deep breaths. The feeling of pins and needles covered my whole body, starting from my back/spinal area to my chest and all over my face, arms, and legs. It feels very similar to morphine except it's more spaced out. Morphine is like a massive rush that hits you all at once, while heroin hits you hard, but its effects last a little bit longer. I switched to H because it's way cheaper than both morphine and hydromorphone. I take a 50mg dose of methadone every day, but I still manage to get high off H whenever I use it.

Once again, I woke up from a very heavy black-induced heroin and Valium sleep to the sounds of Lola crying upstairs. She was crying a little louder than she usually does this morning, and I just figured it was because her boyfriend had probably beaten her up a little harder than usual. But no, there was something about the way her cry sounded. It was slightly different. It sounded like either the worst cry she'd ever had or a cry of relief. Something was telling me it was a leaning toward the relieving side of things. Normally, I don't feel the way I did when I got out of bed this morning. I felt as if it was my responsibility to knock on Lola's door and ask her if she was okay. So, without any second thoughts, I decided to do exactly that. I went outside and lit up a cigarette and smoked for a couple minutes before knocking on her door. I was able to hear that she had stopped crying and that she was putting on shoes and coming down the stairs to answer the door. I heard her footsteps carefully walking down the stairs in an anxious matter. She must've thought that I was her boyfriend or something. She slowly opened the door and saw that it was me and not him.

"Oh…hey," she said.

"Why, hello," I responded back.

"What do you want?" she asked me.

I had to think about it for a minute, but I decided to just shift into the "fuck it" mindset and be as real as I could with her. So I straight up asked her, "I heard you crying this morning. Are you okay?"

She glanced into my eyes with a look on her face that I have never seen before. She looked me straight into my eyes, and every inch of my body was telling me not to blink. Her gorgeous green eyes started tearing up as she finally looked away from my face down toward the ground.

"I'm fine," she replied.

"Are you sure?" I asked, even knowing damn sure that she wasn't fine and that she had been beaten up the previous night judging by the new bruises on her arms and face. "Why are you crying then?" I asked her.

"Oh shit, you didn't hear the noise last night?" she asked back.

"I hear noises every night," I stated. "What was different about last night?"

She looked up and back into my eyes and said, "The cops arrived. Some random neighbor heard him hitting me, and so they called the cops, and they took him away."

I felt very happy for Lola after she had told me that. I felt like not only will I not be kept up all night by the sounds of domestic violence, but Lola is going to be okay now. Or is she?

"Want to come in for tea or coffee?" she asked me politely.

"Sure," I replied to her as my stomach started to fill itself with butterflies.

I went inside and walked up the stairs to her side of the duplex. It was actually very nice inside, and I didn't see any broken or smashed up things. I sat at her kitchen table while she put the kettle on.

"Tea or coffee?" she asked me.

"Green tea if you have, please," I responded.

After she sat beside me at the kitchen table, we both became silent as the kettle started boiling the water within it. It felt very awkward as the only things that I wanted to talk about were all related to her being beaten up every night by her boyfriend. After a few more seconds of thinking, I finally asked her, "Why do you let him do this to you?"

"What are you talking about?" she asked as if she was surprised by the question.

"Why do you let your boyfriend beat you up every night instead of calling the cops or something?" I asked.

"He always says he's going to kill me if I told anyone that he was beating and raping me," she answered.

I almost spit out my green tea all over her face and kitchen table. "He's been raping you too?!" I asked in pure shock.

She then put her cup of coffee down on the kitchen table and put both of her hands on her face and started crying. I felt so bad for her. Such an incredibly beautiful girl getting beaten up and raped every night. How could someone do something like this to such an angel like Lola? Or anyone, period.

"Look, I'm not going to tell anyone, okay?" I told her.

"I don't give a fuck anymore, to be honest with you. I honestly think death would be my best bet by now," she said.

"Well, I can't really argue with that," I said to her.

"What do you mean?" she asked.

"Both of my parents committed suicide, and I've attempted it myself about five to six times but failed every time and woke up in the crisis response center," I answered.

"Both of your parents killed themselves? How did they do it, if you don't mind me asking?" she asked in wonder.

"Well, my dad blew his brains out with his shotgun when I was seven and just over two years ago, my mom rented a suite at the top floor of a

Holiday Inn and smashed her apartment window before jumping out and falling thirty stories to her death," I responded.

"That was *your* mom?!" she answered. "I can't believe that was your mom. I'm so sorry about that."

"Meh, if there's anything I've learned about being alive, it's that life fucking sucks," I answered.

She started laughing a little bit, and I started laughing as well. She had such a pretty laugh. What was she doing that was so wrong that her boyfriend had to beat her up and rape her every night? She seemed like the most innocent heaven-sent angel I've ever seen! Beautiful green eyes, pale white skin, long black hair, and sexy piercings and tattoos. She was fucking perfect! A perfect girl stuck on the furthest thing from a perfect world. Halfway through my green tea that Lola had prepared for me, I took a look at my phone and saw that my best friend since kindergarten who lives in B. C. now had messaged me, asking if I could talk on the phone with him. I texted him back saying I would call him in the next hour or so. Lola finished drinking her coffee and immediately stood up from the kitchen table.

"Hey, you want to have some fun?" she asked with a smile on her face.

Immediately, I thought that she was probably going to suggest something sexual but unfortunately that wasn't the case.

"Come, I have to show you something," she said as she walked away from the kitchen table and went toward her bedroom.

I got up from the kitchen table and followed her into her bedroom. The whole room had a rather sinister feeling to it. As if it was haunted by some evil spirits or something. It didn't help that all the posters she had were all death metal and black metal bands like The Black Dahlia Murder, Cannibal Corpse, Suicide Silence, Burzum, and even Dark Funeral. There were also inverted crosses and small statues of demons. She even had an exact replica statue of the demon Pazuzu from the movie *The Exorcist*.

Lola bent down on her knees and reached for something underneath her bed. After looking around for a tiny while, she pulled out a Ouija board from underneath her bed.

"Wanna try talking to your parents?" she asked.

"Um, sure, why not?" I replied, not feeling 100 percent about the answer I had given her.

"Okay, dope!" she said.

I spent the next ten minutes staring at Lola's face and eyes while she explained the rules of the game to me. I could almost see her aura, and it was magnificently brighter than it usually was. My mom had a gift. She could see people's auras, and her intuition was mind-blowing. When she died, it was pretty much passed on to me. Well, at least the aura part. That's what I think anyway, so fuck it.

Lola and I ended up playing with her Ouija board for the next hour. It was really interesting but also very unsettling and frightening. I started feeling really dizzy after we had made contacts with three different spirits. The first one was named Sharon, and she had died in a car accident when she was twenty-eight. She was friendly, and our session with her was very easy. The second spirit however, Carla, was starting to spook me out big-time. Lola was laughing as if she wasn't taking it seriously, and this spooked me out even more.

Was Lola a witch?! Maybe she was haunting or putting spells on her boyfriend, and rather than burning her at the stake, he beat the shit out of her instead. Who knows at this point? After trying my hardest to forcibly move the planchette to "Good-bye" for a few minutes, Carla gave in and Lola and I were able to squeeze in one more session with another spirit: Anthony. This spirit was the worst of them all. Not only did it blow out all the candles, but it also made Lola's coffee cup explode! We asked if we were still speaking with Anthony's spirit, but the board wrote out, "Zozo" instead. Really bad sign. At this point, Lola was starting to become scared too. Somehow though, she was able to ask the demon when she was going to die. The only reply the board wrote out was, "Tonight." Lola immediately pushed the planchette to "Good-bye," and just like that, our séance was over.

At first, we both laughed and found it pretty funny. But as we kept playing, I could tell that Lola was starting to feel uncomfortable. We both decided it was time to stop, so we both did, and she packed it back up neatly with shaky hands and put it back underneath the bed. I couldn't help but to notice that there was a huge shift in energy in the kitchen that Lola and I were playing in. Lola's skin appeared to get more pale than it already was. She looked at me and then her ceiling. I thought she was just messing with me until her eyes rolled back into her head and she fainted to the floor. I was terrified. I immediately sat down beside her and started calling her name and trying to nudge her in order to wake up. After about two minutes, she woke up looking absolutely terrified.

Chapter  3

"Lola! Yo, Lola, are you okay?!" I asked her as she awoke from a sleepy, trancelike state.

She looked around her whole kitchen before making an attempt to get up off the floor. I offered her my hand, and when she grabbed it, I was able to lift her up off the ground with ease. Her head immediately fell into my chest, and she started crying as she wrapped her arms around my body.

"Lola, what the fuck was that? Does that usually happen to you when you play this game?" I asked her. "Did we break one of the rules?"

"No. I'm not kidding. This is the first time this has happened to me," she answered back.

"Are you serious?!" I asked as I felt another energy in the room and a really bad feeling in my stomach.

"No lie," she said as she sat there with her head inside her arms, looking like she was really tired or something.

"Are you going to be okay, or do you want me to call you an ambulance?" I asked, genuinely feeling concerned about her.

"No, fuck that shit. I'm just going to lie down and try to take a nap or something," she replied with a very weak voice and tone.

"All right then. I'm literally living right beside you, so if you need anything, please don't hesitate to knock on my door, okay?" I told her.

"That means more than you know. Thank you so much, Vincent," she answered back.

I made my way down her stairs, walked outside, and then went back inside my part of the duplex. I locked the door behind me. As I went inside, I felt very freaked out.

"How the fuck did she know my name?" I asked myself.

I honestly don't remember ever telling her my name. How could she have known what it was? I let the anxiety I was feeling take control and immediately went into a panic. Knowing I had a bunch of yellow Valiums left over still in my bedroom, I didn't hesitate to go into my room and chew two of them up. The nice calming effect that it provided was exactly what I needed at that moment. I decided to just lie down in my bed for about ten or fifteen minutes so I could take some deep breaths and really let the Vallies kick in. I was also trying to make sense of what had happened less than ten minutes ago with Lola and her haunted Ouija board. I decided to take a third Valium as I thought of her fainting and being in the state she was in when I left. Why did that happen to her? I hope she didn't get possessed or something. *I certainly hope she's not lying on the floor dead right now*, I thought.

After lying on my bed and having anxious thoughts about Lola, I thought it would be nice to pray for her.

I finished the prayer I sent her, the Lord's Prayer. I usually end all of my prayers with the Lord's Prayer at the end. I figured praying to God for Lola would be a good idea since the Christian/Catholic community heavily frowns upon the use of Ouija boards. They believe that Ouija boards are a way to open a portal/dimensional door and allow demons or even Satan himself to come into our reality. They also believe that people can become possessed by Ouija boards and some of the spirits they conjure up. Very interesting stuff, if you ask me. When I was finished with my prayer, I went outside to have another cigarette. Less than three hours into the day, and I've smoked about five cigarettes. My left lung was starting to hurt pretty badly, so I decided to go to 7-Eleven to buy some Advil.

The warmth of the sun could be felt on my back as I walked even though it was well into fall season. Almost all the leaves I could see on the ground were yellow and brown. My dad used to rake a massive pile of leaves together, and Mom would be holding me close to the pile before softly launching me into it, knowing the leaves were more than enough to keep me suspended from hitting the ground. It was so much fun. The thought of that beautiful memory nearly brought tears to my eyes as I walked on the sidewalk covered in dying leaves. The wind reminded me that today's weather was a little bit cooler than it was back during nostalgia central. Every memory you think of has a kind of glow to it, especially good memories. They always seem very bright as if everything is lit up without the need of a direct source of light lighting them up like the sun. I love walking back through memory lane and experiencing the good old feeling of nostalgia. I'm not sure whether this has to do with the fact that I suffer from borderline personality disorder or maybe because my good memories were genuine. I mean, I had both of my parents in the picture plus an older sister. I'm still grateful for the fact that I'm not some homeless IV meth or heroin bum on the street having to constantly beg people for change all day long. I was very close however. Right before I was accepted by welfare, I had to face the fear of possibly being homeless for a few nights. Thankfully, that wasn't the case. Both my mom and dad had a will plan for us and each other, but since I was the only member of my family left, I had received all the will money. It wasn't a million dollars or anything crazy like that but more so just under a tenth and a half million dollars. I wasn't very happy about it. I would've rather gotten my family back instead of any amount of money.

I placed the tiny bottle of Advil on the counter, and the East Indian behind the till said, "I've seen you before."

"You probably have," I replied in a rude manner.

"No, I mean like on TV!" he said back to me.

"On TV?! What do you mean on TV?" I asked in wonder.

"Yeah, you were in a viral video that made the news everywhere!" he stated.

"What the actual fuck are you talking about?" I asked as I grabbed my bottle of Advil and shoved it in my pocket.

"Surveillance cameras showed you crashing your car in the middle of Corydon Avenue during the early hours of the morning!" he said. "You crawled out of the car, and you didn't have a single scratch on your whole entire body!"

It was at this point where I couldn't make out the words the cashier was saying to me. I got really dizzy, and I felt a sort of flush coming upon me. My vision got blurry, and I remember turning away from the cashier while he was in mid sentence. I felt like puking, so I immediately tried to make my way out of the 7-Eleven, but the cashier started yelling at me in his thick East Indian accent, "Hey! You did not pay for that item!"

"Ahh, whatev…" I attempted to reply as everything became very bright and I fell unconscious to the floor.

I woke up in an all white room wearing a white gown while sleeping underneath a couple of white bed sheets and covers. I knew exactly where I was. I was at the psych ward. As soon as I made that realization, my head started absolutely pounding again. It was as if there was someone both to the right and left of me with baseball bats continuously hitting me in the head over and over again. The lights were super bright, so I tried putting my head under the sheets and try to fall asleep again but couldn't. After a while of trying to fall asleep, I heard the door to my room open. I popped my head out from under the covers and saw a doctor and a nurse with him. They, like everything else, were dressed in complete whiteness. The doctor brought a chair into the room for the nurse to sit in and take notes while he observed me.

"Hello, I'm Dr. Patterson, and this is Dr. Parker," the doctor said. "She is going to be taking some notes while I ask you questions."

"All right," I said quietly as my head was still hurting like hell.

"Do you remember your name?" he asked me.

"Yeah. It's Vincent Caswell," I said back to him.

"Okay, good job! Now, do you remember why you're here today?" he asked.

"Umm, no, not really, no," I answered back.

"Okay, so basically, you experienced a blackout while you were at 7-Eleven," he told me.

"No way," I answered. "I haven't had one of those in a really long time."

"Well, I hate to break the news to you, but that is exactly what happened today. Let me guess, you have a pounding headache right now, correct?" he asked sternly.

"Yes, I do, and it fucking sucks! Can I have some Advil, please?" I desperately asked him.

"We will give you Advil for pain, don't worry about that," he said. "I just need to ask you a few more questions, all right?"

"Okay, fine. Go ahead," I said in an irritable manner.

"Do you remember the last time this happened to you?" asked Dr. Patterson.

"Well, I started getting them pretty much right after my mom died, like two years ago," I answered truthfully. "I think the last one I had was about five months ago."

"Have you ever been treated with antipsychotics before?" he asked before taking a sip out of his coffee cup.

"Yes. I've been prescribed to Seroquel and Zyprexa before. Right now I'm currently on methadone and Valium," I told him.

"We have your medical chart here from your family doctor, and it states that you have been diagnosed with borderline personality disorder, post-traumatic stress disorder, and schizoaffective disorder. Does all that sound right?" asked the doctor.

"Yes, that sounds about right," I answered.

The doctor ended up asking me a few more questions before finally leaving the room with the nurse and promising to be back shortly with some Advil and a prescription for an atypical antipsychotic called clozapine/Clozaril. I really don't like telling people, even if it's medical experts like doctors and nurses, that I have schizoaffective disorder. My doctor tapered me off Zyprexa, which was the last antipsychotic I was on for that disorder. I haven't been on an antipsychotic since then, and that was about four to five months ago. I haven't really been hearing any voices, but sometimes at night I do see shadow people. They're very odd-looking. They're tall, very lanky and skinny, completely black, and they kind of dance/contort their bodies in creepy and weird ways. Imagine being in bed, looking at your black TV screen and seeing that there is someone right beside you, tall, skinny, and black, flailing his arms back and forth kind of like a puppet. Really weird stuff, if you ask me.

By the time I was given a dose of clozapine with Advil and finally out of the hospital with all my belongings, it was already quite dark out. The sun was going down fast, and the darkness around me was growing even faster. I don't live in the prettiest area of the city, so I really don't like being out when it's dark. Thankfully, the psych ward was relatively close to my place, and I thought it wouldn't be too bad of walk back to my place. But I was wrong. I decided to just try and walk as fast as I could before it would become completely black outside.

As I was walking, I decided to check my iPod Touch really quick just to see how far of a walk I had left. It was another good six to seven minutes worth of walking before I'd be walking up my front steps. Then out of nowhere I heard someone stepping on a tree branch and breaking it. I immediately turned around and saw a dark figure on the right side of the street sidewalk and another dark figure on the opposite side. They both started running at me, and boy, when I turned around, I was gone with the wind. I was running so fast as one of the figures behind me yelled, "Yo! Stop!"

I figured doing exactly that would be the worst thing I could possibly do. I kept running like my name was Forrest Gump, and before I knew it, my street had come up. I glanced back for a split second to see if I was still being chased, but I couldn't see anyone or thing behind me. I didn't care though. I kept running like Terry Fox until I was at my front door with my duplex keys in my hands, which were shaking uncontrollably. I finally got the key to unlock the door, and I ran inside slamming the door shut behind me. It was a huge relief to be home and safe. I locked the door and decided to put some heavy weights against the door. But as I walked away from the door, somebody knocked on it.

Chapter

4

I froze with complete fear as someone knocked on my door right after I locked it and put weights up against it. I slowly turned around to face my door and decided to walk toward it very slowly. I then decided to turn around and go into my kitchen to grab a knife in case it was those creepy fuckers chasing me. I started walking toward the door very slowly and bent over to try and move over the weights as quietly as possible. I carefully placed my hand on the lock and unlocked the door, sharp kitchen knife in my left pocket ready to be drawn. I took one long, slow, and quiet inhale as I prepared to possibly attack the person behind the door. I turned the doorknob and swung the door open to see innocent Lola standing there, all alone and looking as harmless as possible.

My heart immediately started racing, not only because of the fact that it was Lola behind the door but also due to her having an extremely abusive boyfriend that does unspeakable things to her.

"Whoa, what are you doing here this late?" I asked, feeling worried.

"What are you doing with that big knife in your hand?" she replied.

"Look, I was just being chased by these two creeps on my way home from the hospital, and I don't know if they managed to see where I live and possibly plan to break in later. Please just come in," I explained to her.

She came inside of my place, and I took her jacket off for her and hung it up on my coat rack by the door. She went straight into the living room with her backpack around one shoulder and sat on the couch.

"Why were you in the hospital today?" she asked me while unzipping her backpack.

"I had a blackout for the first time in a few months," I answered, feeling ashamed about it.

"A blackout?" she asked. "What do you mean by 'blackout'?"

"It's when you experience a massive flow of thoughts that completely flood your brain as the rest of your body floods in anxiety and depression.

I typically lose touch with reality when it happens. It can be really scary and unpredictable because of that," I tried explaining to her.

"That sounds really fucked up," she answered simply.

"They gave me these antipsychotics, and they gave me my first dose less than an hour ago, and holy smokes, I think they're starting to hit me," I said as I all of a sudden felt extremely drowsy and lethargic.

They gave me the second lowest dose at the hospital, and the script they gave me is for the same strength. I felt as if the headache that I had at the hospital was coming back.

"Holy sweet fuck," I said as I sat on a chair in the living room. "They are definitely kicking in now."

"I heard antipsychotics are bad for you unless you actually have schizophrenia," Lola told me.

"Hey, remember when I told you that my life sucked? Well, guess what? I also have schizoaffective disorder," I admitted to her.

"You actually have a type of schizophrenia?!" she asked, looking surprised.

"Yeah. I developed it after my mom died, and I was officially the last member of my family," I said as I wiped off some drool that came from my mouth.

"I think that's really cool," Lola said simply. "You don't seem like you have any psychotic symptoms though."

"Yeah, it's kind of weird because it's not chronic. It just kind of happens at random times, and since it doesn't happen too often, the experiences are typically quite intense. Sometimes resulting in me talking to a crowd of imaginary people," I told her.

"Do you ever hear voices and shit?" she asked. "What do they say to you?"

"They usually tell me to either kill myself or other people," I calmly told her.

"*What!*" said Lola out loud as she pulled her Ouija board out of her backpack.

"Yeah, dude, it's really fucked up. And sometimes they just don't stop, you know? All day long," I said to her.

"What else do they tell you to do?" she asked in wonder, looking like a kid in a candy store.

"They typically tell me to do terrible things like different types of sins and bad shit. They've told me to light Bibles on fire before, vandalize or burn down churches, cut myself, start fights, do drugs," I answered her, now feeling even more tired than in the last five minutes.

"That's some crazy shit, dude," she said to me. "Are you okay? You look like you're nodding off or something."

"Oh yeah, I'm fine it's just my first time taking this new medication," I replied.

As badly as I wanted to tune out from the world and go to sleep because this medication was making me very sleepy, I didn't want Lola to leave. She looked so pretty in her pink-and-black outfit with her long black hair and stunning green eyes. It felt very nice just being around her.

"How do you know that your boyfriend won't come home tonight and beat you like he usually does?" I asked Lola.

"He's not allowed out of jail, even with a bond or bail because he was on probation when he was arrested for abusing me," she answered me.

"Oh, okay. That's really good to know and a massive relief," I said as I laughed a little bit.

Lola went digging into her purse and eventually pulled out a nice jar that contained some quality *Cannabis indica*. She asked if I wanted to smoke up with her, and I said yes.

We sat in my living room smoking Lola's bong. She took about four to five rips whereas I only took about two because I was incredibly groggy from the clozapine. Lola was really starting to notice the effects of the antipsychotic on me and asked if she could sleep over, even knowing that she lives upstairs in the same house as me. I said yes because I was too drowsy to give a fuck about anything and also because I was going to sleep with Lola in the same bed. I never thought in a billion years that something so profound as being able to be close with someone who you really think is special and means the world to you could actually happen.

All right, I'll admit it. I guess I was starting to have a crush on Lola because she was the type of woman where all you really needed to do is get one quick glance to see how beautiful she is and how badly you would like to have a woman like that. I remember we were both in my bedroom, and I was undressing myself as Lola grabbed me with both arms and threw me on my bed and crawled on top of me. I couldn't believe that this was actually happening! A girl that beautiful all over me like this. She eventually got off me and just lay beside me. It took both her and I seconds to instantly fall asleep.

When I woke up in the morning, Lola was nowhere to be found. Did last night really happen or was it just a dream? I honestly couldn't tell at this point. I had a huge headache and immediately reached for my bedside table to grab some Advil. I took three of the extra strengths and decided to lay in bed for a little bit. I grabbed my iPod Touch and saw that it was already 12:15 p.m. I slept in big-time! I felt unbelievably tired and foggy minded. I felt like, if I actually tried, I'd probably be able to sleep in for another two to three hours at least. I had some crazy wild dreams too. Jumping and being able to fly over people's houses, realizing it's a lucid dream and the feeling of excitement that it provides. I really wish I had some cocaine or something stronger than the caffeine, which I had in forms of tea and coffee in my kitchen. I finally managed to sit up, and as soon as I put my hands on my eyes to wipe away the sleep, I heard a knocking at the door. I immediately jumped out of bed, put some clothes on, and went to see who it was. I was really hoping that it would be Lola. I'd love to see her gorgeous face and eyes again, plus that beautiful smile of hers. I opened the door and to my surprise, my neighbor from one house over was standing there.

"Yo, buddy, how's it going?" he asked me.

"Hey, Ronny, what's up?" I answered him.

Ronny is a pretty decent guy although I've had some bad experiences with him in the past when I first moved into the hood. I'm not racist, and I don't hate native people or anything. I've just had some crazy traumatic experiences with them. I've been held at knife point by them about four times; I've had a native stick a handgun into my mouth; I've been ripped off millions of times by them; I've also been beaten up, then robbed, lied to, and also raped a while back by some young native bitches. Yes, believe it or not, men can be raped too; and no, it's not very pleasant at all. Especially when the bitches are ugly. Anyways, Ronny is native and he's stolen money off me and also my old bike awhile back. Since then he's been hooking me up with alcohol or meth every once in a while. It's only when he needs something he comes to me. I was stupid enough to give him money because he said he was going to go and buy me some Xanax with it and asked if he could borrow my bike. Let's just say, if you're stupid enough to allow natives to borrow stuff from you, then you better believe that whatever you gave to them, you will literally *never* see again. And no, I haven't gotten my money or bike, and I know for a fact that I won't.

"Yo, I was wondering if you had a saw that I could borrow off you today?" he asked me. "Here." Ronny passed me a meth bubble with some nice-looking crystals in it.

I grabbed the pipe from him and felt bad about the fact that I may just slip on meth for the first time in a really long time. At least thirteen or fourteen months ago was the last time I used it. He walked into my living room and sat on my couch while lighting up a bubble of his own. I immediately thought, *Fuck it*, and started lighting up my bubble. I felt so tired, and I needed to go to the dope clinic for my methadone and to fill my new script for clozapine. I took more than a few massive hits out of the bubble Ronny gave me and, boy oh boy, was it ever good stuff. I felt all of my tiredness and drowsiness disappeared instantly, and I was hit with a massive rush of euphoria. I felt incredible. I told Ronny to wait in my living room as I went to my kitchen and then straight down my basement stairs to grab a handsaw for Ronny. I spotted one immediately, grabbed it, and went upstairs very quickly. I went back into the living room and handed it to Ronny.

"Fuck, yeah, buddy! This is exactly what I need!" he said in excitement.

"Yeah, no worries, dude. Just try to remember to bring it back, all right?" I asked him, even knowing damn well that I was never going to see that handsaw ever again.

"Oh yeah, yeah, buddy, no worries, man. Thanks so much!" he said as he made his way out of my duplex and walked back to his place.

Good-bye, handsaw, I thought as I stood in the doorway and looked around outside before closing my front door and walking back into my duplex.

I was planning on having breakfast today, but thanks to good old crystal, I had absolutely no appetite anymore. I walked into my kitchen and realized how high I really was. I looked in the mirror, and my eyes were absolutely huge and my skin was a little more pale than usual. My heart was beating very quickly, and all I could think about was last night and Lola. I wondered if she had ever tried meth before. I wouldn't be surprised if she did. I mean, I could tell that she had some experiences with drugs before, especially weed, alcohol, and cocaine. I decided to jump into the shower to wash my hair and body. After doing so, I finally threw my old outfit I had been wearing for the last week straight into the laundry bin and picked out a new one for myself. After blowing my hair dry and putting on my facial cream, I figured I might as well clean since I'm high on meth right now and probably will be for the next twelve hours or so. Having the methadone clinic in mind, I decided to just clean the floors rather than the whole entire place before I go to the clinic.

So after sweeping and mopping all the floors, I put on my shoes and went out the door into another day of autumn. Halloween was starting to get close, and other than summer, I absolutely love Halloween! My mom and dad would always take me trick-or-treating every year, and I would always get a massive amount of candy. Ah, those were the days. As I was walking to the dope clinic, I realized that I had forgotten to call my best friend in B. C. back from the other day. After getting my dose at the clinic, I decided to go straight home and call my friend in B. C.

I called him and as usual, we ended up having a good one-hour conversation. It's funny, sometimes we can go six months or even a whole year without talking, but when we finally speak to each other, it's just like the old days, except I no longer have a sense of humor. Every time we talk on the phone, we always agree that it would be a good idea for me to leave Winnipeg and move to Vancouver, where he lives. I really want to move out there, but apparently, it's very expensive. I would absolutely need to find a full-time job if I wanted to last even a split second out there.

Once I got off the phone, I was feeling very paranoid all of a sudden. I felt like someone for some reason was going to kick in my door and try to kill me. I walked into my bedroom and grabbed my bottle of Valium. I immediately picked up two tabs and put them in my mouth in order to chew them up. It felt very nice and relaxing. I decided to lie on my bed and read. I was reading the medical notes that came with my prescription of clozapine, and it sounds like the worst medication ever! Especially when it comes to the side effects from it. I didn't really want to start on another medication anyways. Maybe it will help me, or maybe it won't. Time is going to be the one with the answer when it comes. I lay there, and when a couple of minutes passed, I heard someone knocking on the door. I started feeling paranoid again and very worried. I took a deep breath and opened the door to see pretty girl Lola standing there.

"Hey," she said to me.

"Why, hello there," I replied back to her. "Would you like to come inside?"

"Absolutely!" she said in a British accent, which I found surprisingly funny.

I was so happy to see her as she made her way inside my place.

Chapter

Most people say that meth can make you feel more horny and perform better in bed. I, however, completely disagree because it turns my dick into a flat tire. Nonetheless, I thought it would be a good idea to just not mention the fact that I had used the drug, in case Lola never used it before and would think of me only as a meth head tweaker. I highly doubt she likes me back considering how beautiful she is. Having borderline personality disorder, it's very easy to fall in love with anyone. People with BPD like me feel emotions stronger and longer and more intensely. It's a really shitty mental health disorder, and it typically makes most of its targets feel suicidal and shit. Really terrible disorder but somewhat manageable with dialectical behavioral therapy mixed with SSRI antidepressants and atypical antipsychotics.

"So guess where I just came from?" Lola asked me.

"Upstairs?" I answered.

"Ha ha ha. No, I just came back from the psych ward," she said to me.

"You were in the psych ward just now?!" I asked her, feeling surprised.

"No, silly head. My crazy once-was boyfriend is in there, and he's lost his mind," she explained. "The security guards had to pull him away from me when I wanted to leave."

"Holy crap! Did he try to attack you?" I asked her.

"Kind of, yeah. He didn't want me to leave, and he wanted me to try and convince the guards that he's not crazy, but I didn't want to, and when I said no, he grabbed me with both arms, and I remember feeling frozen, but the guards grabbed him within seconds of him grabbing me," she answered me.

"I thought you told me that he was in jail?" I asked, feeling a bit confused.

"Yeah, he was for a bit, but then they did some psychiatric shit on him, and he's locked up in the psych ward now. He kept telling all the doctors, nurses, lawyers and just anyone in general that I was evil and that he was protecting the world from me," she said.

"He said he was saving the world from you? Well, you are a pretty badass bitch," I replied.

"Oh, shush," she said while laughing. "But yeah, really fucked-up shit."

"That's like so random and weird. Why does he think you're evil? Did you play Ouija with him too or something?" I said, laughing.

"All jokes aside, yeah, I did actually play with him a few times. He didn't really like it, and it scared him like crazy, ha ha," said Lola, still laughing a bit.

"Well, if it makes you feel any better, I definitely don't think you're evil in any way. I think you're an angel," I said, immediately biting my tongue as hard as I possibly could after. Did I really just say that to her? Damnit, she's going to think I'm in love or something, and it's going to be awkward now, fuck! Why did I say that, fuck!

"Awh, Vincent that's so sweet," said Lola as she blushed a little bit.

A huge feeling of relief followed.

"Yeah, he must have been seriously schizophrenic or something because that's a pretty wild story, I must say. That sounds worse than my schizophrenia!" I said, chuckling a bit.

"Coconuts, if you ask me," agreed Lola.

"So what are your plans for the rest of the day?" I asked her.

"I was going to ask you the exact same question, to be honest," she admitted to me.

I was thinking about asking Lola if maybe she wanted to go out for a walk to the park or out to get ice cream or something, but I was worried about being rejected. Either way, high as a kite of good old crystal meth, I conjured up the courage to do so.

"You want to go for a walk in the park or something?" I finally asked her.

"Sure!" she said with a smile on her beautiful face. "Is it okay if I bring something with me?"

"Yeah, go for it! I have to grab my jacket from my room anyways!" I told her as I made my way to my room. My jacket wasn't in my room but my wallet was, and I thought maybe I'd ask Lola if she would like to get some ice cream or something. I heard her leave my place, closing the door behind her and then walking up her stairs into her place.

My heart was racing. I couldn't believe that I was about to spend a bunch of time with Lola! I can only imagine what people will think seeing a guy like me walking with a woman like her. Not that I care, but still, somewhat interesting to think about. I then heard her walking down her stairs, so I hurried myself up and made my way to the door. When I walked out, I saw Lola standing there all pretty and waiting for me. I smiled at her when I saw her, and she did the same to me. I turned around and locked my door, feeling the happiest I've been in forever.

"All right, let's do this!" I said to her as we walked down the front steps of our shared duplex. "So what was it that you had to grab from your place before we left?"

"Oh, you know, this thing," she said as she pulled out just enough of her Ouija board so I could see it.

Damn, she and I have chilled three times in total, and every time, she brings her Ouija board with her. This is a little bit strange to me. The second time she pulled it out, we didn't even play because I was too fucked on antipsychotics, but still, she brought it.

"Oh my god, you're bringing that thing with us?" I said to her, making a funny look on my face.

"Yeah, you said that we're going to the park, and there's a cemetery there!" she told me, looking all excited and shit.

"We're going to play with that fucking thing in a cemetery?! Dude cemeteries are resting places, not hospitals where mothers give birth!" I told her, laughing a bit.

She laughed really hard right after I said that to her. "They're a perfect place to play the game because you can always communicate with a spirit," she said to me.

"I thought your half of the duplex was more than enough?" I asked sarcastically.

"Oh, ha-ha, very funny!" she said sarcastically, rolling her eyes at me.

"There's a church there too. I don't know if they're going to be happy to see a couple of shitheads playing with a Ouija board on top of some random bastard's grave," I said to Lola.

"Oh, stop being such a pussy, Vince," she said to me, smiling.

"What can I say? You are what you eat," I retaliated back, laughing.

"Wow, I cannot believe you just said that," she said, before practically folding in half from laughing so hard.

The park was only about a twenty-minute walk away from our duplex, and it was a very nice day outside. The way the sun shined off the yellow leaves in the trees, and the way it reflected off Lola's long silky black hair was magnificent and almost magical. It was such a perfect day, and it felt as if time didn't even exist. In fact, it felt very psychedelic and spiritual in a way. It felt like the plateau of a really good acid trip. Where you feel like you're completely connected to the universe in an oceanic way. Feels like everything is just water and you're connected to everything. I love LSD, but not as much as this day though. At least so far.

We walked through the park and made our way to the cemetery. It wasn't a very large cemetery, but it was beautiful and the upkeep was always in perfect condition. I used to go to this church with my whole family, but now that I'm alone, I don't bother going at all. We walked through the entrance gates and walked to a corner of the cemetery where there were a lot of trees, and we decided to sit right underneath it. Lola pulled out her Ouija board, and we both placed our hands on the planchette.

"You ready?" asked Lola, a massive smile on her face.

"Better believe it," I replied in confidence.

Even though I did feel a little bit worried about what might happen. I mean, we were in Lola's place and shit got absolutely crazy, so I couldn't imagine what was about to happen if we played in this cemetery. As soon as Lola placed her haunted Ouija board on the leaves and grass, the wind started blowing relatively hard. I also noticed that there were clouds forming over the nice blue sky that was once there. Now I was starting to feel uncomfortable and a little bit frightened.

"All right, let's get this show on the road!" said Lola.

"Are you sure we should be playing this game in a cemetery?" I asked Lola, noticing my voice was a bit shaky.

"Hell, don't be worried about it, it'll be more fun than it was at my place," she said, laughing a little bit.

"Okay, what should I do if you start convulsing or pass out again? Crush up some pill and put it under your tongue?" I said, kind of feeling like a dick about the way I said it after I said it.

"I'd prefer if you could plug it for me," she said calmly, obviously trying hard not to grin.

"And what exactly is it that I'm plugging you with?" I asked, being so close to laughing out loud.

"A 150mgs of Adderall, extended release," Lola said, finally laughing.

"Oh wow, I didn't think you were the type of person who was into anal beads," I said, now finally laughing myself.

"I feel really bad for this dead bastard that we're sitting on top of," Lola said.

"Same here, we haven't even asked the board any question, and I bet we've already pissed off more than a few spirits!" I replied.

"More than a few at least," said Lola as she finally focused her attention on the board. "Hello, Ouija, are you there? Is anyone there?"

As soon as Lola finished saying the word "there," the planchette flew out from under both of our hands and landed on "Yes."

"Okay, that was really fast, " said Lola, looking blown away.

We both put our hands back on the planchette and tried playing again.

"What is your name?" asked Lola.

At first, nothing happened but then the planchette wrote out, "You know who I am."

"Are you Zozo?" Lola asked very briefly.

"No, my name is Saint Edwin," answered the board. "You better run."

"Who better run?" Lola asked the board.

"Lola," the board answered, and Lola and I looked up at each other.

"Okay, so that's really fucked up, don't you think?" I asked Lola.

"Why do I have to run, and who exactly am I running from?" asked Lola with a bitchy tone in her voice.

"It's me who you're running from, and you know exactly why," answered the board.

"Okay, this is getting really fucked up. There's some spirit coming after you, and you're not even afraid?" I asked Lola in a worry.

"I know this jackass. He's the one who framed my ancient ancestors for being witches and had them burned at the fucking stake!" answered Lola, looking at the board as if she was going to pick it up and start punching it or something.

"Are you fucking serious?!" I asked her in a state of shock.

The clouds above us turned dark, and all of a sudden, the sound of thunder was near.

"Lola, this is actually crazy! Look what's happening with the wind and shit," I said to her, still feeling very uneasy about the situation.

"I'm pretty sure this is the one, Vince. This is the ghost of the man who framed my elders and had them killed," she said to me calmly, disregarding what I had said about the wind and stuff.

"It looks like it's going to start pouring at any moment in time now," I said, trying to be as calm as she was.

"Are you rotting in hell yet?" Lola asked the board in a rude tone.

"Did you seriously just ask that to a Ouija board? Lola, this thing is going to kill us or drive us both insane!" I stated. Then looking over Lola's left shoulder, I could see a crypt with both of its doors opening from the inside. At first, I thought it was haunted until I saw people dressed up in all black robes coming out of it and their leader coming out in a red robe wearing a goat mask on his face. The other men dressed in the black robes all had balaclavas so you couldn't see their faces. Then the goat leader, or whoever he was, pointed at Lola and me.

"Holy shit, we have to leave now!" I said, trying stand up as fast as possible.

"Vincent! You can't just take your hands off the planchette like that!" she said to me, sounding rather upset.

"Turn around!" I yelled at her.

She turned around and saw the creepy cult-looking group of people running at us at a fast pace.

"Holy shit!" said Lola as she grabbed her board as quickly as possible, putting in her purse, and then turning around and running away with me.

"Who the fuck are they?!" I asked Lola, sprinting right beside her.

"Don't waste your breath and just keep running!" she answered back to me.

Lo and I ran out of that cemetery as fast as possible, and the weird people stopped running after us once we were off the church property.

Chapter 6

Even though the weird cult people stopped running after as us soon as they reached the boundary between church soil and the street, I was scared beyond belief! Lola and I were being chased by some crazy Satanist cult members! They saw exactly what we looked like, and who knows who they were? They could've been anyone from a priest of the church to someone who just sits in the back during Sunday morning service. The fact that the leader in all red was wearing a skeletal mask of a goat was by far the scariest part. As soon as I saw that mask, I knew they were satanic. Lo and I kept running way beyond the church and straight into a 7-Eleven where we managed to catch our breaths.

"Okay, that was really, really fucked up," I said, panting heavily.

"Who the fuck were those guys?" Lola asked, also panting, trying to catch her breath.

"I was hoping you would know," I replied to Lola.

"They must have been some underground Satanist cult operating underneath the church or something," Lola stated.

"I don't know who they were, but I'm surprised I didn't literally shit my pants during that getaway," I said to her in odd confidence.

"Yeah, that would've been shitty," said Lola in an edgy tone.

"I think we should go back to our duplex. What do you think?" I asked Lola.

"Sure. Let's just try to keep a look behind our backs as we go there though. Those ass hats could've jumped out of their jumpsuits, and we don't know who was underneath them. They could be anywhere or anyone," Lola tried to warn me.

"All right, I'll keep a lookout behind us if you have the front covered. Cool?" I decided to ask her.

"Okay, sure. Let's get a move on then," she replied in confidence.

We left the 7-Eleven after loathing there for a little while and made our way back toward our duplex. The dark clouds that once occupied most of the sky had dispersed, and the wind had died down. It looked as if the sun was also going to come out again, but for some reason, I had a really bad feeling in my stomach. We got close to the 7-Eleven that was very close to my place, and I told Lola that I had to go behind the building because I was going to puke.

"Are you serious? Right now?" asked Lola, looking surprised.

"Yeah, dude. I feel like I'm gonna explode, and I don't want to do it in front of you," I said to Lo as I ran behind the Seven feeling extremely nauseas and very lightheaded. I projectile vomited all over the back wall of the innocent 7-Eleven. I felt bad, but it felt so good puking all of this up. It felt like a different type of puke. It felt like I was puking out negative energy rather than the large amount of liquid I was really puking up.

"Oh my god, are you okay?" asked Lo as she cautiously peeked around the corner to see me.

I was barely conscious but somehow able to hold myself up, thanks to the wall.

"Well, I do feel a lot better than I did before," I said to Lo in all honesty.

"Are you sick or something?" she asked with a very worried look on her face.

"Honestly, Lola, I have no idea. I need to go home and lie down. Today has been really fucked up, and I just want to lie down and hopefully drift off into a nice slumber," I answered, even knowing that I was still high on meth and I wouldn't be able to fall asleep for a while.

"Okay, I understand. I think I'm probably going to do the same thing, to be honest," she answered, genuinely looking concerned about the state that I was in.

"All right, let's make our way then," I said back to her, feeling very weak and still dizzy.

We walked back to our duplex and said our good-byes at our front door.

"I hope you feel better Vincent because I want to hang out again," she said, smiling and looking into my eyes.

"Oh, I will. I just need to lie down for a little while, and I'll feel better in no time," I said once again, knowing I probably wasn't going to fall asleep considering I had used meth today.

"See you later," said Lola while lunging in and giving me a kiss on the left cheek.

I literally couldn't believe it! Lola just kissed me! My heart starting beating very quickly, and I developed a gnarly erection.

"Bye, Lola," I said, trying to maintain my cool, which I wasn't doing very well considering how fast my dick jumped up when she kissed me.

I went inside my place feeling like one of the luckiest guys in the world. I can't believe that Lola actually kissed me! What an absolutely perfect day with a perfect ending to it! I was still pretty high from the meth I smoked earlier in the day too, but it was starting to wear off, and I could tell because I was starting to feel shitty and tired. This is the reason why I never became a full-blown meth addict. I don't understand how people can manage to just keep doing it for like five days without sleeping or eating while being all paranoid and delusional. I started feeling more and more paranoid as the hours went by. I don't know why, but I keep thinking about those guys who chased me a couple of days ago and those weird satanic people who chased Lola and me. I kept thinking that they knew where we lived, and I feared that at any moment, they can break in and murder me and Lo, or at least rob us. I managed to remember to take my clozapine and Valium, and I figured that once the antipsychotic kicked in, my paranoia would be gone. It didn't work the way I imagined it would, but it knocked me on my ass and made me tired enough to fall asleep. The dreams I had that night were beyond fucked up. Dreams of Lola and I being tormented by demons and sinister creatures, and the usuals about Mom and Dad.

Chapter 7

I woke up feeling like absolute shit. It was about 2:30 p.m., so I figured it had been close to a full twenty-four hours since the meth had entered my body. Either way, it normally takes a good four to seven days to completely exit your body depending on your metabolism. I lose weight like crazy whenever I do meth. My metabolism is already higher than any ceiling, and I honestly lose weight overnight. If I go a full day without eating anything while high on meth, I can seriously lose about one to three pounds in a single day. Pretty fucked up, right? Anyhow, I got out of bed after spending half an hour on my iPod looking up DMT and other weird third-eye stuff. I jumped in the shower because I woke up all sweaty, and my sweat smelled like meth. I still didn't have an appetite but figured that I would force myself to eat. I had a bowl of Cheerios alongside two pieces of toast on the side. I still felt somewhat paranoid and on edge from the ice I used yesterday. I decided that maybe for once, I can finally sit down on my cushion and meditate for a little while. I set up everything inside of my spiritual room including crystals, incense, a couple of candles; and I even put my headphones in and managed to find a video on YouTube for relaxing rainfall noises. I was sitting comfortably with my legs crossed, hands in my lap, eyes closed; and I even let out a massive fart beforehand so I wouldn't have to hold it in during my spiritual healing process. I took my first few breaths and tried keeping my attention on the in and out of my breath. Then all of a sudden, *bang, bang, bang*, someone was knocking on the door. For fuck sakes…I didn't even care if I was about to open my door and maybe see Lola. I genuinely felt sick, and I was really starting to get into that meditation that I started. Really pissed off, I stood up from the cross-legged position I was sitting in on my meditation cushion and made my way to the door. I opened the door to nobody standing there, but instead, there was a mysterious box on my front step with no stickers or logos. It was just a plain brown box lying there. I didn't get a chance to see who had dropped it off for me, and the parcel didn't even have my name or address on it.

This is really weird, I thought. I don't even remember buying or ordering anything online, unless I did order something online but my memory was wiped from that meth that I smoked yesterday. So standing there as curious as a cat, I picked the box up, went inside, and locked the door behind me. I decided to go straight into my living room after grabbing a knife from the kitchen to cut open the mysterious box. Then, when I finally sat down on the couch with the box, it hit me. Maybe this was one of those random mystery boxes from the darknet! The only problem with this is that I know I haven't ordered anything from the darknet for a really long time and this may be one of those traps where inside the box there's a murder weapon and then seconds later, the cops show up and arrest me. After making that horrific realization, I started feeling very nervous about opening this box. I had no idea what I was going to find in it and whether or not is what from the darknet. After debating what to do for a little while, I decided to just crack open the box to see what was inside. I opened it, and there was some packaging on top, but once I removed the white packaging, I saw that there was a really weird-looking book inside the box. Just looking at the book made me feel very uneasy and somewhat nauseous. I grabbed it and took it out of the box and placed it on my lap as I sat on my couch. Only moments ago, it was sunny and gorgeous outside, but when I cracked open the box and pulled the book out, it got very cloudy, very fast. I started feeling the way I did when I was with Lola at the cemetery and we got chased by those weird-ass people. It then sort of hit me that maybe whoever dropped it off knocked on the wrong door and that this package is probably for Lola.

Yes! This makes so much more sense now, I thought as I put the book back inside the box with some of the packaging and made my way outside to knock on Lola's door. After knocking a few more times, it was obvious to tell that she wasn't home. So I decided to just turn around, sit on my front step, and light up a cigarette while looking at this fucked-up book. After lighting my Camel Blue, I pulled the book out of the box again and opened it to the first page where I could barely read some writing. All I could read was, "Written by Lo, for those who don't know." What the fuck could that possibly mean? Maybe there's more inside. I decided to open the book down the middle, and the first two pages I saw scared the shit out of me. There was writing, but it was in an alphabet I've never seen before, and all of the texts were written in some kind of red ink. I really hope this isn't blood…because I've had hepatitis C before and it sucks. I got the cure for free, but if I manage to fuck up and get infected with it again, I'll have to pay some $60,000 for it, which is a bit beyond my budget, to say the least. Anyways, looking at these pages was almost starting to put me into a minor trancelike state. I couldn't read or understand any of the writing, and the pictures inside were horrific. There were pictures of different types of demons like Zozo and Beelzebub plus what looked like instructions on how to cast black magic spells. The pictures of children murdering their parents messed me up the most.

I need a fucking drink! I thought. So I put the book down on one of the footrests in my living room and went into the kitchen. I opened one of the top cabinets above my sink and pulled out a nice glass and then headed to the fridge. I opened the fridge and pulled out a two liter of cola with about half of it left and a bottle of Jack Daniels with at least four to five shots remaining. I didn't bother with the ice because my bottle was already really cold from being in the fridge, so I just mixed the two together and then decided to go pop a Valium before coming back to that terrifying novel. When I finally got back to the living room, I literally stopped in my tracks and froze so fast that a sip of my drink accidentally spilled on the floor. I left the book open and on top of my footrest; and now, all of a sudden, it was on my couch and closed…

That is rather fucked up, I thought. I took a big swig of my drink and walked over to my couch where I sat down and placed my drink on the floor. Feeling more nervous about the book than I had before since it literally moved on its own, I decided not to obsess over it and just flip through it very quickly. It had a hard cover and back cover, and the texture almost felt like it was made out of tree bark while the pages were almost as soft as Kleenex. I started slowly flipping through the pages, and I got to say, this is hands down the most sinister thing I have ever been around, other than Lola's Ouija board with all due respect. So many pages contained depictions of angels falling from heaven and into hell, 666 all over the place, the seven-headed dragon Baphomet, Satan, inverted crosses, and even people killing themselves. Boy, this is really messed up. I wonder who wrote this book and when they wrote it, and why. I put the book down on the couch beside me and decided to go back to my room to grab my laptop and do a little bit of research on this shit. I left the living room and was about to walk through the kitchen when halfway through, I heard a sound come from my living room. It was as if something fell or something got knocked over. Feeling paranoid now, I slowly made my way back to my living room to see that the demonic book was now lying on the ground.

"You got to be fucking kidding me right now," I said to myself. I put my drink down on the windowsill and went to pick up the book. Right before I grabbed it, *bang, bang, bang*, someone knocking on my door again. This time I wasn't irritated; this time I was absolutely terrified! I was hoping that maybe it was going to be Lola and she would be able to explain all of this paranormal nonsense. I went to my door and opened it to one of my friends who I haven't seen for a really long time. Her name is Lizzy, and we kind of used to have a thing a couple of years ago. I don't think we actually dated or anything but we used to hang out and hook up all the time. Sometimes we wouldn't even hook up and just listen to music while tripping balls off of LSD, shrooms, or even ketamine.

"Vincent! Oh my god, it's so good to see you!" she said, looking all excited with the biggest smile on her face.

"I literally can't even remember the last time we chilled, Liz. I missed you!" I said as we both lunged in to hug one another. "Please come in."

"Why, thank you," she said before making her way inside.

"I'm honestly really glad that you came over, Lizzy," I said, thinking about the demented book I was scrolling through.

"Oh yeah? And why is that, Vince?" she said with a grinning smile on her face.

"Okay look, first of all, let's catch up. How have you been? What's new?" I asked her.

"Well, do you remember when I was working at Walmart?" she asked me.

"Yeah, I do remember that," I said to her. "Why? Are you still working there? I thought you said you hated that job though."

"Yeah, I hated it up until about four months ago," she answered with confidence.

"Oh, let me guess, you got a promotion?" I questioned her.

"A little bit, yeah. I'm a fucking manager now though, bitches!" she said, throwing up her hands in celebration and accomplishment.

"You're a fucking manager?! Wow, that's one hell of a promotion! I bet it's easier and more laid back than your previous position, yeah?" I asked Lizzy.

"Holy shit you have no idea, Vince. Now I'm the one who gets to boss people around and tell people what to do while I basically look over and make sure that they don't fuck up," she said, looking as if she was really proud of herself, which I imagine she was.

"Dude, congratulations! That sounds so solid. You're probably raking in more cheddar, hey?" I asked, cracking a smile.

"Oh hell, yeah! I'm responsible for getting everyone's paystubs all in order and shit," she replied.

"Wow, that's awesome news! However, I forgot to ask (which I honestly did), did you want tea or coffee or anything to drink?" I offered her.

"Sure! I'll have some black tea like orange pekoe or English breakfast," she answered.

"Nice choice. I was going to make the exact same beverage for myself too," I replied.

"Oh, wait!" she quickly said right as I turned around to get going into the kitchen.

"Yeah, what's up?" I asked her as I turned around to face her.

"What the hell is this thing?" she asked, holding up the demonic book.

"Oh, yeah. That's some book that showed up on my front steps today. I wouldn't look through it if I were you," I warned her.

"Ha-ha, I'm not scared of this thing," she said as she cracked it open.

I turned around and went into the kitchen to set everything up for the tea.

"How do you take your tea?" I yelled from the kitchen.

"Two milk and two sugar, pretty please," she said.

I started boiling the water and realized I had forgotten my alcoholic drink on the windowsill in my living room. I went back into my living room to see Lizzy sitting on the couch with the book open between her lap. Her jaw absolutely dropped. I went over to the windowsill to see that my drink wasn't there anymore somehow.

"Looking for this?" asked Lizzy, holding up my glass, which used to have a drink in it but was now completely empty.

"Um, yes. I was hoping it would be still full, but I don't blame you. I made that drink because of that book," I explained to her.

"Okay, well, turn the kettle off and fuck the tea. I have cash on me, I'll pay you if you give me a couple drinks," she tried offering.

"I think that makes more sense than tea, right?" I asked her sarcastically.

"Absolutely, Captain Obvious," she said back to me, standing up to hand me the empty glass.

After I had made two drinks in the kitchen for Liz and me, I went back into the living room and popped a squat right beside her. She was looking so good. She looked like she had been working out or on a diet or something because she really looked great. Her hair was done perfectly as well as her nails and toes. Her legs were what got my attention the most though. They were sexier now they had ever been before. My goodness, what a beauty.

"Dude, this is some fucked up shit right here. I don't even understand anything in this book, but it's so fucked up and tormented," she said while slowly looking over some of the pages of the satanic scriptures.

"Hell, tell me about it. The package it came in didn't even have a name or address on it either," I informed her.

"Do you think maybe it was for the crazy couple living upstairs?" Lizzy asked me.

"That's what I was thinking, so I went to knock on the door, but there was nobody there," I said.

"Really? Okay, because when I was waiting on your front step, I looked up and saw some chick standing by the window looking at me. She had very pale white skin and long black hair covering most of her face. Kind of like *The Ring* or that movie *The Grudge*," she answered with a confused look on her face.

"Wait, what? You mean like, just now? Just a few minutes ago?" I asked her, feeling very surprised.

"Like less than ten minutes ago, yes, sir," Lizzy answered me.

"What the actual fuck! I knocked on her door half an hour ago, and nobody answered," I said to Lizzy.

"Maybe they just finished fucking or something?" Lizzy asked, smiling.

"No, her boyfriend got arrested a little while ago because some neighbor heard him beating her. If anything, I would've heard Lola finger blasting herself or at least using a dildo," I replied.

"Well then, shall we go over and try knocking?" asked Lizzy, looking all excited.

"Sure, let's do it. I'll bring this demonic bible with me."

Lizzy and I then made our way to the door to put our shoes on.

Chapter 8

After we put our shoes on, we went outside and both lit up cigarettes to smoke before knocking on Lola's door. We decided to sit on the front step and talk until we were finished with our smokes.

"So do you still go on the darknet sometimes?" asked Lizzy.

"Yeah, sometimes. I'm starting to believe that maybe this demonic book was a surprise mystery box from the darknet," I replied.

"That would make sense for sure. There's some crazy fuckers out there," she said.

"Why do you ask? You still using ketamine?" I asked as a smile formed on my face.

"Ha-ha, no. I only smoke weed and drink occasionally nowadays. I went to rehab again just over a year ago, and since then I've been successful. How about you? Are you still pinning dope?" she asked me after answering.

"Not really. I mean, I do sometimes, but it's not a daily thing like it used to be, you know? I'm still on methadone too, and other than that, just weed and liquor," I answered back.

"Oh, that's good to hear! I remember how badly dope was starting to ruin your life, so I'm very happy about that news!" she said, looking genuinely happy.

She leaned in and gave me a big hug. We both then stood up afterward and threw our cigarettes onto the street after butting them out. I walked up to Lola's door and knocked four times. After standing and waiting for a while, I decided to knock a couple more times. Neither Liz or I could hear anyone inside or coming down the stairs. Liz and I looked at each other.

"You said you saw someone up there?" I asked her, feeling somewhat uneasy.

"Yeah! It was some albino emo-looking bitch with long black hair," Liz responded.

"This is really bizarre," I stated.

"Why don't you just check and see if her door is open?" Lizzy asked me.

"Hmm, that's not a bad idea at all," I said as I put my handle on her doorknob.

I turned the doorknob, and to our surprise, it was actually unlocked! I saw that Lola's favorite pair of Converse shoes was at the bottom of her stairs, and she wears those everywhere.

"Fuck! What if she hit her head or had a seizure or drug overdose?" I asked Liz in a sudden panic.

"Well, fuck, let's go upstairs then!" Liz said as we both made our way up the stairs and into Lola's duplex very quickly.

I was shocked. There was nobody home! Lizzy and I looked around everywhere but didn't find anyone inside the duplex. We even checked the closets too.

"Okay, so now I'm really creeped out," stated Liz. "This is actually impossible. I know I saw some chick up here looking at me through the window on this floor."

"I'm just as freaked out, if not more. It was just yesterday that I was hanging out with her too," I replied to Lizzy.

"Do you know if she has beef with anyone?" Lizzy asked me.

"Beef?" I asked her.

"Yes, beef. Like drama. Enemies and shit? People looking for her possibly?" she asked me.

It was right at that moment when I made a huge realization. Maybe it was that fucked-up cult from the cemetery! Or maybe she's just out, who knows?

"Dude, her room is so fucked up! I mean, look at all this satanic bullshit everywhere. Holy fuck! I'm not even religious, and I can honestly say that this is some fucked up shit right here!" said Lizzy, who was in a state of surprise and wonder.

"Pretty sinister, hey?" I asked Liz.

"Very sinister, Vincent. Very sinister indeed," she answered back.

"Just try to maybe not move anything around. I don't want her to think that someone walked into her place and robbed her or something, you know?" I stated.

"Oh my god," said Liz from Lola's bedroom.

"What?" I asked Liz.

"Vince, I think you better come and take a look at this," said Lizzy in an uncertain voice.

"What's going on?" I asked Lizzy as I walked into Lola's bedroom.

"This shit right here, bro, check it out," said Liz as she passed me what looked like a diary or journal.

"Lola told me not to look into her diary when I was here a few days ago, so I don't feel comfortable about this," I responded.

"Yeah, but you're already invading her property at this very moment, so what difference does it make?" she asked me.

"Okay, fine. Pass it over here then," I said to Liz.

She passed me the diary, and I opened it to the most recent page, which was a journal entry that contain nothing else but my name written over and over and over again. I started flipping through all of her entries, and they were all the same. "Vince" and "Vincent" written absolutely all over the place, and the more I focused my attention on the diary, the more dizzy I became. I got so dizzy that I eventually dropped the diary on the floor and leaned on a wall.

"Do you two know each other well or something?" Lizzy asked, looking at me with a smile and a wink as a way to suggest that perhaps Lola and I had sexual encounters.

"Not really, no," I replied.

"Oh really? Because that diary seems like she has 24/7 access to sitting on your face all day long," replied Lizzy, laughing and nudging me on my shoulder with her fist.

"No, seriously, I'm not kidding! This is so fucked up. We have to get out of here before she gets home and finds us trespassing on her property!" I replied cautiously, urgency behind my statement.

"Oh, come on, you party pooper! This shindig is only getting started!" said Lizzy as she pulled a flask out of her purse and took a shot out of it before giving it over to me.

"Gee, thanks, Liz," I said as I took a shot from the flask and passed it back to her. "Oh, shit! Is that gin?!"

"Yes, it is! Why? Do you like gin?" she asked me as she took one more shot before putting it back inside her purse.

"I absolutely hate it with a burning passion!" I exclaimed back at her.

"Oh, perfect. More for me then!" she said, starting to laugh.

"More like the rest is all for you because I can't stand that shit!" I said to Lizzy.

"Even better!" she said, genuinely looking very happy about it.

Then all of a sudden, we both heard a very hard knock/pounding on the door below. We both immediately looked at one another and simultaneously put our hands over our mouths. I nodded my head toward Lola's bedroom as the loud knocking continued. We both made our way into Lola's room, and I pointed for Lizzy to get down and go under the bed. As she made her way to that very location, I heard the door being opened and realized that we hadn't locked it when we came in. I looked around and finally decided it best if I hide in Lola's closet. I quietly made my way into the closet and got comfortable behind some clothes. I peeked out a bit to see if Liz had full coverage, and she did. Lola's bed had bottom curtains on it, and Liz was hidden perfectly. I decided to try and shut the closet door a little more than it already was and really get deep inside. The footsteps were extremely loud. As if each step was stomped on in a very aggressive manner. I felt so scared, and I was covered in sweat all of a sudden. I heard Liz weeping underneath the bed, so I quickly pulled my iPod out of my pocket and texted Liz, saying, "*Be quiet! They're almost upstairs. Did u put the diary back?*"

She texted me back seconds later, saying, "Yes, I did. I'm so scared right now, Vincent!"

I texted her back, saying, "It's going to be okay, just be dead quiet, and this person will leave eventually!"

The person had now gotten to the top of the stairs and was inside Lola's place. I couldn't really get a good look out the closet without making any noise or blowing my cover, so I just stayed put. I could hear the person walking around very slowly as if they were investigating the place or something. I heard them walk throughout the whole place and then realized that this person was headed for the room we were hiding in. I became extremely anxious, and my heart started beating very rapidly. I saw a person covered from head to toe in a dark black cloak just walking around Lola's room. I was so shit scared I thought I was going to shit myself! Or at least let out one of those long, wet nervous-sounding farts that smell like a cannibal's puke after eating a rotting human corpse. I tried to keep my eyes on the phantom-like being and saw that it was attracted to Lola's bed. The dark figure then started bending over as if to check if there was anything under the bed where Lizzy was! SHIT! What do I do? I started looking around the dark closet I was inside of and saw that there was a baseball lying on the floor. I quietly bent over to pick it up, and when I did, I pushed the closet door ever so slightly open a bit, stuck my arm out, and threw the baseball out of the room and into the kitchen. I did it in one swift motion, and I'm glad because as soon as the baseball hit the floor, the being shot up from almost being completely hunched over to standing straight in a millisecond. It was insane! The way it made its way out of the room didn't really look human either. It was so fast and odd when it moved. Either way, it was out of the room and I could see it in the kitchen holding the baseball in one of its hands. It then turned around to almost faced me perfectly face-to-face from across the duplex, but I managed to lean back into the closet in time. As about another minute passed, we heard the strange being starting to make its way down the stairs. I started to breathe way easier, and I felt so fucking relieved. We eventually heard the door shut, and then we both slowly came out of our hiding spots.

"Okay, who the fuck was that, Vincent? Was it her? Was it Lola?" Lizzy asked frantically.

"No. No, it wasn't. It was something else," I said to her.

"What do you mean something else?" she asked me.

"It was some person in an all-black cloak, but the way this person moved was so fucked up! It was all contorted and bizarre looking. That's the best way I can explain it," I said, trying to sound as honest as possible.

"Okay, well, whatever it was, it left. And now I think it's time for us to leave as well, hey?" Liz said to me.

"That's a fantastic idea! Let's do that like now," I said as we both made our way to the stairs.

We got to the bottom of the stairs, and I quietly opened the door and poked my head out to see if there was anyone watching. My eyes didn't see anything out of the ordinary or any strangers who could've possibly been watching an invasion of property brought to you by Lizzy and me and brought to you in part by some creepy apparition. We made our way back into my side of the duplex and decided to just sit for a little while and finish our drinks I had made earlier for us.

"That was so fucked up! Are you serious, it actually tried looking under the bed?" Liz asked, looking very afraid.

"I swear to god, yes. Did you hear that bang outside of the room? I threw a baseball into the kitchen right when it was about to lift the bottom curtains on the bed you were underneath," I explained to Lizzy.

"Vincent, are you serious right now?" asked Lizzy, becoming really serious all of a sudden.

"No lie whatsoever! I'm not even trying to make up a fake hero story or anything, I swear. That thing was about to grab those curtains and reveal your whole body, so I panicked and looked around the closet and managed to find this baseball that I instantly picked up and launched in the kitchen," I said, feeling really proud of myself.

"Really?" she asked again, a little less serious this time.

"Yeah, why?" I asked her.

Then all of a sudden, out of nowhere, Lizzy attacks me by grabbing my face and pulling it toward hers and started making out with me like crazy! Literally out of nowhere, a huge make-out sesh that very quickly led to the two of us to race each other to my bedroom. I let her beat me in the race and literally… We were on top of my bed before I knew it, and Lizzy's top vanished. Her knockers looked wonderful! I mean, they always did, but like I said earlier from an examination, Lizzy looks better than she ever has in her whole life! She was on top of me for a good half hour before we decided to go doggy style, my absolute favorite! Also, according to the Chinese calendar, I was born on the year of the dog, so…yeah. Guess it was meant to be. Anyways, doggy lasted a good forty-five, and then we 69d each other until we both came, and my oh my, whether I'm on medication or not, I produce an inhuman amount of semen. Like if you were to see an amount I produce on a good day with a partner that I'm very attracted to, you wouldn't believe that it was all my own, considering Liz and I have had more than a few sexual encounters together and we know how to really satisfy each other. We both know each other's bodies so well that we know exactly what to do with one another. We only had a thing for so long, but it was really good now that I think about it and especially after that orgasm!

"Holy fucking shit," said Liz as she lay beside me in my bed and lit up a cigarette.

"Oh, can I steal one of those off you, pretty please?" I asked her kindly.

"Here." She just passed me her pack with her light, and I got one going for myself. I love cigarettes after sex—in general and the music group too.

"Fuck, that was awesome. I came so fucking hard when I was on your face, I almost screamed!" said Lizzy as she laughed a bit and continued taking long drags of her cigarettes. The reason why I asked for hers even knowing I have mine was because I wanted a designer cigarette. Lizzy buys Belmonts, and they are *not* cheap. Just over $20 for a pack of twenty-five nowadays. But whatever, they taste great!

"Yeah, same here. I'm really glad you moved your face before I erupted everywhere," I said to Liz with a huge grin on my face.

"Thanks for having my back at your girlfriend's possessed apartment. It really means a lot, Vinny," Liz said shortly, before giving me a huge kiss on my left cheek.

"I got your back like chiropract! Courtesy of Andre 3000, ladies and gentlemen!" I said to Liz with a straight face, looking deep into her pretty blue eyes.

"Ha ha ha! You're ridiculous you know that, Vinny?" said Lizzy as she stared back into my eyes.

Oh, Vinny, that's the nickname that girls give me when they like me more than a friend. I noticed it back as early as elementary school. And ever since, I've been able to tell whether a chick is into me. Now that I think about it, I really wish that Lola would start calling me Vinny. I can believe this craziness! I've been chilling with Lola like crazy, and now Liz drops back into my life for the first time in a while, and boom, we have sex just like that. Am I gonna have sex with Lola? Lord knows I desperately want to, yes. Even just oral alone! I'd go down Lola for like two days straight if she'd let me. That's always been my specialty and go-to: eating pussy. I just really enjoy it. I find it very naughty, especially when the female is a little bit younger than the guy going down on her, like teachers eating high school senior year cheerleading pussy during detention. That's always been my go-to. But enough of my sexual desires.

"What are your plans today?" I decided to ask Lizzy.

"Absolutely nothing, and I swear to god, I was just about to ask you the exact same thing," she said, finishing up the rest of her cigarette.

"I'm not doing anything either. You want to go for dinner and drinks or something?" I asked Liz in confidence.

"Fuck yeah!" said Liz all excited now. "Where do you want to go?"

"I was thinking maybe something like Earl's or Moxies maybe? They're relatively affordable, and it's great food," I answered to Liz.

"Do you like Olive Garden by chance?" Lizzy asked with a huge grin on her face.

"Oh hell, yes, I didn't even think about that one! I haven't been there in a long time either, so if that's what you're thinking, then I'm 100 percent on board with you, darling," I said, grinning back at her.

"Yay! This is going to be awesome! I'm going to call them now and set up a reservation. What time should we be aiming for? Right now it's almost four p.m.," Lizzy told me.

"Want to do six or six thirty?" I asked.

"Sure, let's do it up!" said Liz, looking even more excited than before.

Lizzy then called Olive Garden to make reservations for us while still lying naked next to me in my bed. Her body was magnificent! Not that it wasn't before but damn! I'm thinking yoga and exercise. Lizzy got off the phone after making a reservation for 6:30 p.m.

"So I was wondering?" Lizzy asked me.

"What's that, pumpkin?" I asked her.

"You, um, wouldn't be able to go down like one last time before we put our clothes on?" she asked me in a very flirty voice.

"I was starting to think that you'd never ask!" I said, getting off the bed, grabbing Liz by her ankles, turning her body to me, and pulling her to the edge of the bed.

I instantly got down on my knees while she played with my dick using her bare feet. It got me so turned on that I spread her legs wide open real quick and began my feast. It took just under four minutes for me to make Lizzy cum again with my tongue. And boy, was she vocal during this climax!

"Jesus Christ, you are so good at that!" said Lizzy, looking like the most satisfied woman on the face of the earth.

"It just turns me on, and girls really enjoy it whether you're great at it or not. As long as I get to eat pussy, I don't even require a return favor," I explained happily to Liz.

"Well then, time to get dressed and grab some dinner!" said Liz, still excited as hell about dinner and drinks. I mean, I'm the one who brought it up, so I'm assuming that she thinks I'm paying for the whole thing… ah, whatever, that pussy was too good!

It felt so good to finally have sex again for the first time in a long while. I isolate myself so badly and don't even bother trying to talk to girls or even use dating sites and shit. I'm pretty self conscious about the way I look. Not that I'm fat, but the exact opposite literally. I've always been a good thirty to forty pounds underweight. I'm six foot one, and I weight just over 120 pounds. The most that I've ever weighed was about 143pounds, and I *still* looked anorexic as hell. Pretty fucked up shit, if you ask me. I had also completely forgotten about the meth I used yesterday and how shitty I felt today from it. I'm so happy that Liz decided to pop by. I remember being in love with her and telling her so, only for her to say she's crushing on some other guy. Didn't really matter though because whether she was in a relationship or not, we always hooked up and fucked anyways. We both got dressed and were ready to go for dinner.

"So did you maybe want to smoke up before we go?" I asked Liz kindly.

"Oh, fuck, yes! Let's get high right before dinner. What should we do until then?" she asked me with such a cute look on her face.

"Do you want to go for a walk? Or shall we stay here and look through the darknet?" I asked, laughing like an evil villain.

"Let's do the darknet but without that supervillain laugh because the darknet is scary enough alone," Liz replied.

"Fair enough," I calmly replied back.

I left Lizzy in the living room as I went back to my room to grab my laptop. I came back and sat down right beside Liz on my couch. I opened my laptop and powered it on. It only took me a few minutes, and just like that, there we were, on the darknet. Looking through tons of horrific content, most of which Liz wasn't handling well, so I decided to just go to the drug content. Liz was absolutely blown away as she was viewing these pages with me. Lizzy and I ended up spending a good hour browsing through the darknet, and we even made an order for some ketamine to use when we hangout again, which, for the record, I'm really looking forward to considering how today worked out… We found a weird page with strange symbols on it and written instructions on how to enhance human abilities. It had a lot written about people's auras and interesting scriptures about how there will be a new worldwide currency and economic system.

Both Lizzy and I were very interested in this discovery we had made on the darknet. We kept looking through the pages on the website for a long while and almost lost track of time.

"Holy shit! Vin, look at the time!" said Lizzy as she pointed at my clock on the wall.

"Oh, damn son! Good thing you brought your whip!" I replied back.

"You know it, Vince," she said to me with a smile on her face.

"I'm really looking forward to this food!" I said as we left my place.

"Oh shit!" said Lizzy as she stopped in her tracks and turned around to face me.

"Please don't tell me you're cancelling last minute or something," I said while purposefully making a sad face with long lips.

"No, of course not! We forgot to get stoned, and we have to leave like immediately!" she said, looking disappointed now.

"Okay, that's no problem, bro! I'm going to run to my bedroom and roll a joint really quick, and then we'll smoke it on the way there," I said as I turned away from her to face my front door.

"I'm going to come with you," stated Liz.

"For fuck sakes, you want to cum again?! You're something else you know that, old sport?" I said to Liz, trying to keep a straight face. It was difficult.

"You sick bastard! I'm going to knee you in the balls if you don't hurry up, Gatsby!" she said back to me while softly pushing me toward the door.

We both got inside got went straight to my room without even taking our shoes off. I immediately opened my real life-size treasure chest full of all my drugs that aren't prescribed to me. I grabbed my grinder, which already had a whole bunch of weed chopped up inside of it, and put it on my desk with a pack of Zig Zag Blues. I pulled a paper out and opened my grinder up. Then I grabbed a whole bunch of weed and stuffed it into the one paper.

"I don't know if that's going to fit," said Liz as she watched me do my magic.

"That's what she said!" I replied calmly.

"No, seriously. That's a massive amount of kush for just one paper," Lizzy tried explaining to me.

"Believe me, old sport, I have mastered the craft of rolling black dildos," I said back to her, all while perfectly keeping my composure and rolling an absolutely massive joint almost bigger than the size of my own fucking pinky!

"How in the fuck did you do that! Wow, that's incredible, Vin!" said Lizzy, sounding very surprised and impressed.

"I told you so, old sport," I replied as I realized the Great Gatsby trolling might've been overdone a bit.

"Come at once, Gatsby! Let us fly ourselves over to the Garden of the Olives," she said back to me, surprising me big time.

We then left my place very quickly and made our way over to Lizzy's car and got inside of it. I put my seat belt on before pulling a lighter out of my pocket to light up the cannon of a joint I rolled up in less than a minute. I started lighting it up as soon as Lizzy drove her car away from the curb she was parked at, and the car started filling up with smoke. The joint couldn't have burned any better. I hate it when I light a joint up, and it starts canoeing, or even worse, kayaking.

By the time we got to Olive Garden, the joint was already a small joint and we both decided to toss it out of the window before parking in the parking lot. We got out of the car, and we literally just barely made it for 6:30 p.m. We walked into the restaurant, and Lizzy told the girl working that we had reservations. The hostess then asked if we were Lizzy and Vincent, which both of us agreed to, and then followed her to the table that we were going to sit at. We were seated and handed drink menus before the hostess informed us that a waiter was going to come by soon with the food menus.

"So what's your poison tonight, Liz?" I asked as I started looking at the drink menu.

"I think I'm going to order me a Caesar," she replied.

"Oh, that actually sounds really good!" I said to her as I had my attention on the wine section. I usually don't have wine unless I'm eating steak, but for some reason, I was craving it.

"Here, let's see that menu," Liz said.

"Here you go, mango," I said to Lizzy as I passed the drink menu over to her. I had made my decision about the wine, and it was a go.

For some reason, I, all of a sudden, had a really weird feeling down deep in my stomach. Was this my intuition, passed on from my mom, trying to tell me something? I wasn't nauseous or anything, I just had a short, but very sharp pain, in my stomach. It kind of felt a little bit like the stomach pains I would get when I had hepatitis C but not as long and consistent. I started thinking about the decision I had made with the alcohol and realized that wine probably wouldn't be the best for me to have. Something that's not acidic. Rum! I'll have a rum and Coke.

"So you were kidding about the glass of wine, right?" asked Liz.

"Oh yeah, it was bullshit. I'm getting a rum and Coke, instead," I answered her.

"That sounds more like you. Also, I wanted to ask, if I may? Why are your pupils so dilated?" Lizzy asked me with a concerned look in her eyes.

"Oh, I had a little bit of a slip yesterday. I hung out with Ronny, and he gave me his bubble with a massive shard in it, so yeah. I felt like absolute shit until you came over and then came all over my face," I said, producing a huge smile.

"Oh my god, shut up! There's children here with their parents and shit," said Liz.

"Fuck them, ha ha ha," I said, failing to keep my composure and not laugh.

"You're so bad. You know that?" Lizzy said to me.

"Better believe it, girly," I said back.

Then, just like that, as soon as we went silent, my stomach started having these small pains again. What the fuck is going on here? I put both of my hands on my stomach and tried to massage it a little bit.

"I can see that someone's hungry!" said Lizzy as she looked at me rubbing my stomach.

The waiter finally showed up, and we ended up ordering our drinks.

"What can I get for you to drink tonight?" the waiter asked Lizzy.

"Oh, I will have a Caesar, please, and thank you!" Lizzy replied.

"Sounds good! And for yourself, my friend?" he asked me.

We don't even know each other, and he's calling me "his friend."

"I would like to grab a classic rum and Coke, if that's all right?" I replied to him.

"All right, perfect! I'll come back with your drinks and breadsticks, and for now I'm going to pass these menus on to you," he told us, before passing both Lizzy and I a menu.

"Thank you," I said.

"Thanks!" said Lizzy as she seemed very excited to receive her alcoholic drink.

"So what's Lizzy craving tonight?" I asked her, even knowing that it was kind of a stupid question considering how we just got the food menus now.

"I'm really craving fettuccine, to be perfectly honest with you," she said as she could clearly see it on the menu. "How about yourself?"

"I can't remember what it's called, but it's a four cheese something. I get it every single time I come here," I answered.

"Oh, I think I know what you're talking about," replied Lizzy.

"Yeah, it's really delicious," I said back as I saw the waiter walking toward our table with both of our drinks on a platter. He made his way up to our table and placed the platter down on it.

He gave us another couple of minutes to decide, but we didn't even need it really. It felt like the more time that had passed, the worse these stabbing pains have gotten in my stomach. They weren't consistent, which was good, but they kept coming in small doses. I tried my hardest to keep my cool because I didn't want Liz to be worried or have to drive me to a hospital or something.

"I'm going to go hit up the bathroom, I'll be right back," I said as I got up from the table and made my way toward the washroom.

It was as soon as I walked into the bathroom that I realized that I had forgotten to go and take my dose of methadone at the dope clinic. Fuck, this is seriously bad. I don't want to get dope sick, but then again, I've gone about three to four days without my methadone in the past and never became dope sick, so maybe this won't be all that bad. Plus maybe I should text my friend and get some heroin off him if I truly start feeling ill. I decided to take a piss since I was in the washroom anyways and then ended up texting my friend. He responded, saying that he had some really pure stuff that he could sell to me. Feeling a bit more relieved now, I left the washroom and went back to the table where I could see that both our drinks had already arrived.

"Did you bust a quick nut in there or something?" asked Lizzy, smiling at me.

"Nah, my balls turned into raisins after I almost nutted on your face," I said to her while clinking my glass against hers.

"That poor sticky ceiling of yours…," replied Liz.

"That ceiling's a champion! I've never seen anyone or anything take more loads than that. That ceiling has taken more loads than your local Laundromat," I said, finding it hard not to laugh at least a little.

Lizzy broke down finally and started laughing too. We ended up finishing our drinks quickly and had to order another round for ourselves. We were having a really good time, and I could tell that perhaps it wouldn't be over after dinner. In total, we ended up having four rounds of drinks with our food, and at this point, it seemed like Lizzy was going to end up spending the night at my place. And you know what that means, right? Yeah, I thought so. Liz and I both stumbled back to her car and started driving back to my place.

Chapter 9

"I can't believe we ate that whole dessert!" said Lizzy.

"I can't believe I didn't clog their handicap toilet!" I said.

"Ha ha ha, you're fucking crazy," she said to me, laughing.

"That's schizoaffective to you, bitch," I replied back to her with a purposely sassy tone.

"Boy, you best watch that mouth of yours, before I put my customized vibrator in your bum hole!" she threatened, grinning.

"I've always wondered if that would feel like the exact opposite of taking a shit, which sounds shitty no pun intended," I revealed to her.

"Imagine if I turned it up to *full* capacity and speed," she said.

"Holy shit," I replied.

"Oh yeah, you don't want to go there," she said.

"Hell, nah. I'd rather go to hell," I replied.

"I think the overall ride and experience would be a lot smoother in hell. Maybe a little hotter, but smoother," explained Lizzy.

"I don't know about you, but I'm going to roll and smoke up another joint when we get back to my place," I said to her.

"Oh, fuck yeah! Count me in on that shit!" said Lizzy.

"Is it just me, or are you also seeing a lot of cops?" I asked Lizzy, feeling really worried all of a sudden.

"Yeah, they're all passing us and going in the exact same direction as us too! Holy shit, what do you think is going on?" asked Lizzy as she seemed worried now too.

We finally drove up to my place, and we were both absolutely shocked at what we saw. There were about three cop cars parked outside the front of my place and another two cruisers parked behind my place, all five of which had their lights on. I saw Lola standing in the front yard of the duplex, and even my neighbor Ronny was out on his front lawn smoking a cigarette. I thought maybe for a second that Lola had noticed that Liz and I went into her place, but the front door of my place was open and there were cops coming in and out of it.

"What, the, actual, fuck, " I said as I stared in disbelief at what I was seeing.

"Holy shit, what the fuck happened here?" Liz asked, also having her eyes glued to the scene.

Liz and I got out of her car and walked up to the duplex.

"What the fuck happened, Lola?" I asked her as my eyes started tearing up.

"Look, I don't know how to tell you this, but someone broke into your place, and when I say 'broke in,' I really mean broke in... As in, they broke in, robbed the place before breaking everything and leaving. I'm so fucking sorry, Vincent," Lola said as her eyes started tearing up too.

"Well, where the fuck are they! I'm going to pay these cops enough to let me curb stomp these little bitches!" I asked her in a state of emotional frustration.

"Excuse me, sorry to interrupt your conversation," said one of the cops as he walked toward us. "Do any of you happen to be the person who lives on that side of the duplex?"

"Yupperz, I do," I said, slowly allowing the feeling of shock completely take over my whole body.

"Okay, well, I hate to be the one to inform you about this, but it looks like somebody broke in, stole some possessions, and destroyed your place," the officer explained to me.

I have borderline personality disorder, so my mood is either black or white with no gray middle. I can go from being in the happiest mood to being completely suicidal in less than minutes. And that's exactly how I felt while looking at my now completely destroyed place. Liz started talking to the officer with Lola while I just decided to walk past them and go into my place. Everything became silent. All the officers were talking, but I couldn't hear anything because I was about to black out. I walked around my destroyed place, and the only thing on my mind was running into the kitchen, grabbing a knife, and cutting my jugular wide open and dying. All of my family pictures had been ripped and smashed up; my furniture had been torn up; my TV was stolen along with my laptop, guitar, *and* my skateboard. I looked around for my weed stuff, and all of that was stolen too… Suicide has never sounded better before in my whole entire life. I started hearing voices, but they definitely did not sound like any of the officers. They were coming from inside my head, and they were reminding me to kill myself considering I have nothing to live for. At this point, I kind of felt like I've never had anything to live for. My whole family is dead, so why not join them, right? Like mother, like father, like son… I was walking out of my trashed place to sit on the front steps and smoke a cigarette when I started feeling my thoughts spiralling into each other and my legs gave out right underneath me. I ended up falling down my front steps face first and smashing the side of head on the railing before hitting the concrete and completely blacking out.

"Holy shit! We need a paramedic here!" screamed Lizzy as she saw a small pool of blood emerging from my split open head.

"Vincent?! Vincent, are you okay?!" shouted Lola as she kneeled down beside me.

"We're going to need a paramedic over here!" yelled one of the officers into his walkie-talkie.

I woke up on a beautiful island. I was lying on a beach towel, and I had no idea what happened, who I was, or where I was. I looked over to my right and saw my mom and dad walking toward me. I looked over to my right and saw my sister walking toward me. They all started running toward me, and I started crying so hard because I couldn't believe what I was seeing before my own eyes. My mom, dad, and sister all hugged me at the exact same time; and the four of us all turned into one beam of really pure, bright beautiful light. I closed my eyes, and when I opened them again, I was in a place that was very white, clouds all around, and I felt very happy and content. I was with my whole family. I think it must have been heaven or something because we were all laughing while talking and having a great time! We all started talking about how stupid life is and how much better death is. My family told me that I can explore the whole world in seconds as an "orb." I didn't really care because I hate planet Earth and I've always wanted the world to end anyways so everyone can suffer the way I have suffered my whole entire life. I was so happy to be with my family again. The euphoria I was feeling was similar to the happiness I experienced on a regular daily basis before God took my whole family away from me. Fuck God. Fuck everything. I want to stay here for the rest of infinity.

"I never thought I would see you guys again!" I said to them as I kept crying uncontrollably.

"We are always with you, Vincent. And you can be with us if you choose to," my father explained.

"What do you mean? I'm with you now, and I'm not fucking going anywhere!" I said back to him.

"We're trying to help you, Vincent. End your life and join us before your soul gets stolen!" my mom said to me, a smile on her face.

"We miss you so much, Vince. Please join us," my sister said to me.

"I'm here though. I'm here right now! I'm not going anywhere else!" I answered them.

"Not for too much longer unfortunately, my son," said my father.

"Why? Why not? Why can't I stay? I want to be with you. I don't want to leave this place!" I screamed in disappointment.

"Vincent," my sister said.

"Vincent, are you there?" said my mom.

"Yes! I'm here! I'm right here!" I screamed at them.

"Please join us, Vincent. Please, before it's too late!" my father said to me. "You know what you have to do. Leave that evil world you live in and join us."

All of a sudden, everything started fading away. My family members were all starting to float away from me and everything was starting to become black. I could feel sadness, emptiness, and disappointment. I was literally just with my whole entire family until, all of a sudden, everything just faded away. I opened my eyes, and I saw two doctors dressed in all white hovering over me as I lay on a bed in the psych ward.

"*Nooo! Fuck this shit! Nooo! Fucking kill me right now! Please fucking kill me right now!*" I screamed at the two doctors.

"Here, pass me the injection," said one doctor to the other.

My Stupid, Sad, Pathetic Life

"Please! Please fucking kill me right now. I don't want to be here anymore. I want to be with my family again! Please kill me. I'll give you $100,000 if you kill me right now! Please do it, please!" I kept begging them.

"Vincent, we're going to give you an injection of Invega Sustenna. It's going to hurt a little, but it'll only last a minute or so," said one of the doctors.

"Fuck you and your antipsychotics! The only injection I want is a lethal one! And I need that shit right now, bitch!" I yelled at her.

It wasn't until I tried moving my arms and legs that I realized I was tied down to the bed. I screamed so loud and probably made a really big scene in the hospital, but I didn't give a fuck. I was just with my whole family, and just like that, they were all gone, and as usual, I was all alone again. I didn't even feel the injection, but I did feel the effects on me. I went from going absolutely crazy and screaming very loudly to being a zombie in seconds. I even started drooling out of my mouth a little bit.

"Now we're going to give you a dose of lorazepam, Vincent," said the doctor.

"No! Please I really don't want that right now," I said back to the doctor.

"You're going to need some sleep, Vincent. You banged up your head pretty badly when you fell, and you have a minor concussion," the doctor explained to me.

"Okay, fuck it. Give me it so I can fall asleep and be with my family again," I replied.

"What do you mean, back with your family?" asked the nurse.

"Why do you guys think I freaked out the way I did when I woke up? I was literally in heaven with all my dead family members, and it was the happiest I've ever been since I was with all of them at a very young age. I thought maybe I finally died and I could be with them already instead of living this stupid, pathetic life of mine," I explained to the doctor and nurse as I started crying. I couldn't stop thinking of the experience I just had. It really was heaven,

"We're very sorry about what happened with your whole family, Vincent. We really are. And we're also sorry that you have to be here in this hospital, but we just want to make sure that you are safe and okay. All right,

Vincent? It's almost 12am so I'll get my assistant here to go and get that dose for you, and then you can have a good night's rest!" said the doctor.

"All right," I replied shortly before they both got up and left the room I was in.

The nurse eventually came back but this time by herself, without the doctor. I was feeling extremely sedated from the injection I had received and knew that no matter what dose this lorazepam was going to be, I would fall asleep quickly.

"Okay, so along with the Ativan, I brought Tylenol and Advil, just in case you have a headache. How's your head feeling, Vincent?" she asked me very kindly.

"I do actually have a bit of a headache now that you mention it. Can I have a little bit of both Tylenol and Advil, please?" I replied.

"Of course, Vincent. So here's a regular-strength Tylenol and a regular-strength Advil with some water," she said as she passed me a small cup of water with a small paper cup containing both Advil and Tylenol. "Now for the lorazepam, just place the tablet underneath your tongue and it should dissolve quickly."

"What strength is this, if you don't mind me asking?" I asked as I noticed the tablet was an oval shape, which must've meant it was a 2mg tablet.

"It's 2mg," she replied.

"All righty then." I felt happy because 2mg is the highest dose that Lorazepam comes in. The antipsychotic they injected me with was starting to make my legs feel very restless, but I knew the lorazepam was going to take that away in a matter of minutes.

"Is there anything else I could get for you before you go to sleep, Vincent?" she asked very kindly.

"I think I'll be all right for now. But I do have a question if you mind?" I replied as the tablet was dissolving quickly.

"Absolutely! Fire away," she said.

"What do you think happens when you die? Do you think you get to see your lost loved ones again?" I asked her.

"That's a pretty big question, Vincent. With a lot of complicated but possible answers," she replied. "I believe that people can go to a variety of different places in the afterlife based on their actions in this current life."

"Where do you think you're going to go when you die?" I asked the nurse.

"Well, I don't entirely know to be honest. I just hope I get to see my husband again. He died last year from lung cancer after we were together for almost thirteen years," the nurse explained to me calmly.

"I'm very sorry to hear about your husband passing. Was it related to smoking, if you don't mind me asking?" I asked her.

"He had never smoked a day in his life. He worked at a nuclear power plant, and sometimes he wouldn't wear his breathing mask. I would always text him, trying to remind him to always wear the mask no matter what, but he didn't listen to me. The doctors found a lump in his lungs, and they said it was directly related to nuclear waste exposure," she said while trying to hold back her tears.

"Damn. Once again, I'm very sorry to hear that. I hate losing loved ones," I said to her.

"It's not easy for anyone to lose someone close to them. It really leaves a lasting impact on the rest of your own individual life," she said to me.

"I couldn't agree with you more, nurse," I said to her, and she smiled back at me.

"All right, I'm going to let you have some rest now, Vincent. Tomorrow in the morning you will get reevaluated and based on that, the doctors will be able to judge whether you can leave right away or if you'll need to stay here a few days for further examinations, okay?" she explained to me before walking to the door and turning off the lights.

"Sounds good to me. Thank you, nurse," I said.

"I hope you have a great sleep, Vincent, sweet dreams," she replied as she smiled and walked out of the door.

They had untied me from the bed after giving me that dose of Invega, so at least, I'd be able to sleep on my sides. I felt so much better now that the Ativan had kicked in. I crossed my fingers as I fell asleep as good luck. Maybe I could see my family again when I fall asleep! Guess I'll see in a few minutes…

Chapter 10

I woke up to the sound of heavy laughter. My eyes were open and my mind was awake, but I couldn't move my body at all. I couldn't see a direct source of light, but the environment I was in was beautiful—gorgeous green grass, trees, and a terrific blue sky above. There didn't seem to be a sun in the sky, but yet everything was very bright and perfectly lit, as if everything in this environment was glowing. I was finally able to feel my arms and legs and able to wiggle my fingers and toes. I managed to sit up and saw that I was lying in a beautiful field of grass. Looking ahead, I could see my mom, dad, and older sister sitting and lying on the grass underneath a beautiful big tree. They were all together, and they each had rainbow auras and halos above their heads. I tried calling out to them, but they couldn't hear me. Eventually, they all turned their heads toward me and started calling me over.

"Vincent, sweetie! Come be with us!" my mother said to me, smiling and laughing.

"My son! It's been too long! Come sit with us in paradise," my father said as he waved me over to sit with him and the rest of my family.

"I'm coming, you guys!" I screamed to them in relief as tears flooded my eyes.

I managed to stand all the way up and started making my way toward the tree my family was sitting under. They all looked so happy and even happier to see me. I felt so happy as I was making my way to be with them. As I started to get close to them, I felt someone or something grab on to my ankles, and all of sudden, I couldn't move forward toward them anymore. Whatever had taken hold of me, stopped me from progressing forward and eventually pulled me back with a very strong hold. I hit the grass hard and started being pulled away from my family by my ankles.

"Come back, Vincent! You know how to, sweetie," my mom said to me.

"Nooo!" I screamed as I was being pulled away.

My whole family started getting further and further away as the demonic force holding me by my ankles was pulling me away at a very fast rate. I finally found the courage to turn around to see what exactly was pulling me away from heaven into hell. I was absolutely shocked by what I saw when I managed to turn around. It was Lola, an extremely demonic-looking Lola to say the absolute least. Her whole body was scratched up and contorted while her eyes were oil black and her teeth were that of a werewolf or wild creature. I looked into her eyes, and everything went still.

"Please, Vincent, don't leave me here all alone. You're the only one in my life who cares about me, and I can't stand the thought of losing you," Lola said as she slowly turned back into a normal-looking human being without any demonic features.

"Why did you pull me away from my family, Lola?" I asked her in confusion.

"Because you were about to die, Vinny. And I can't let that happen because I need you," she explained to me.

"Why can't we just end it together then? And be in paradise together with my family," I asked Lola.

"It's all lies, Vincent. Everything you just saw was bullshit. That wasn't really heaven, it was just the devil playing tricks on you!" Lola tried explaining to me.

"Fuck sakes. How do you know all this?" I asked her.

"I've been fooled many times by the devil, Vinny," she said to me. "It's very easy for him to manipulate, lie, and take advantage of you."

"Where are we right now?" I asked Lola.

"We're in your dreams, Vincent. However, now it's time for you to wake up and save me! Please save me, Vincent!" she begged as the dream ended.

I had a couple more dreams before finally waking up. They were very similar to the first two I had about my dead family. Dreams of me being young again and being with them for what seemed like a lifetime. I also had more dreams about Lola begging me to stay and "save her," whatever that meant. I woke up feeling very groggy and incoherent. I lay in the hospital bed with a minor headache, trying to remember and repeat the dreams I had of my family. They were all slowly starting to fade away, but

I didn't care. I kept trying as hard as possible to make sure I would never forget about those divine dreams and visions I had experienced. I heard a quick knock at the door before a doctor and nurse made their way inside.

"Vincent Caswell?" the doctor asked as he looked at me.

"The one and only," I replied as he stood by the bed and the nurse sat down on the bed beside me.

"How is your head feeling this morning, Vincent?" asked the doctor.

"It hurts a little bit for sure. Pretty minor compared to last night," I said to them.

"Okay, we'll get some Advil for you right away. We just need to check your vitals and examine you for a little while. Chances are you're probably going to have to stay here for another day. Is that okay with you, Vincent?" asked the nurse.

"Well, I don't really have anything or anyone to go home to anyways, so I can stay here for the rest of my life, I guess," I answered.

"We're very sorry to hear about the break-in, Vincent. However, there is someone here who's been waiting to see you for the last couple of hours," said the nurse with a smile on her face.

"First, we just have to ask you some questions, all right?" said the doctor.

"Wait, someone is here to see me?" I asked in disbelief.

"Yes, there's some people here waiting to see you," said the nurse.

"Well, tell them I'm awake and bring them in here already," I said in a rude tone.

"Don't worry, we will. Now do you remember anything from last night, Vincent?" the nurse asked me.

"I remember yesterday being one of the best days ever until it turned into the worst day ever," I explained to them. "My friend and I were drinking a bit and smoking weed, and then I remember coming home and then I don't remember shit to be honest."

"You know that you blacked out and hit your head, which resulted in a minor concussion correct?" the doctor asked this time.

"Yeah, apparently that happened," I replied.

The nurse and doctor took turns asking me different types of questions. Some of which were easy and others that were difficult, not only because I couldn't really remember shit but because I remembered that my place had been broken into and trashed. I find it so strange that nobody was able to see or hear these people who broke in. I also don't understand why they had to trash the entire place while they were already stealing very valuable possessions. Fucking assholes. I swear to God if I catch these dirty little fucks, I'm going to kill them! Shortly after the doctor and nurse left the room, both Lizzy and Lola entered and gave me a hug, one after the other.

"Vinny! Oh my god, are you okay?!" asked Lizzy even though she probably knew that everything wasn't okay and wasn't going to be for a long time.

"Vincent, I'm so sorry this happened to you," said Lola. "I came home after hanging out with an old girl friend of mine and saw what happened to your place. I also noticed that they came inside of my place because I forgot to lock my door. I thought my place was going to be ransacked too but for some reason, it wasn't."

Lizzy and I both glanced at each other for a second when Lola said that.

"Are you fucking kidding me?!" I said angrily to make it seem like I didn't know what Lola was talking about. "They broke into your place too, but they didn't even take anything?"

"Here's where it gets really strange," said Lola. "When I got to the duplex, your door wasn't actually kicked in or broken, and neither was mine…"

"Wait, what do you mean?" I asked her.

"It's like, whoever 'broke-in' didn't actually break in. It's as if they just walked into both of our places. I know this because when I went to turn my doorknob, it was already unlocked," Lola tried explaining to me.

"That's impossible without having keys though," I said to her.

"Yeah, here's the really shitty part. As soon as I got to my friend's place, I had a really bad feeling in my stomach. Like intuition wise, you know? I had this horrible feeling that I had forgotten to do something and right at that moment the idea of me possibly forgetting to lock the door to my place," Lola explained.

I knew exactly what she was talking about because I had felt the exact same feeling she was talking about when I was at dinner with Lizzy: the stabbing pains right in the center of the stomach. I felt like I had forgotten to do something and then in the bathroom at Olive Garden realized that perhaps it was because I missed my dose of methadone. But I was wrong. I guess I must've forgotten to lock my door when Lizzy and I were in a rush to make it to our dinner reservation on time. Fuck me!

"For fuck sakes! I had that feeling too. I knew something bad was going to happen," I said as I let out a long sigh.

"What feeling?" asked Liz, giving me a funny look.

"When we were at dinner together and I got up to use the bathroom, I had a horrible feeling in my stomach, exactly like the one Lola was describing just now," I explained.

"Wait, you guys were at dinner together?" Lola asked, looking a bit upset.

"Yeah, we were at Olive Garden, and it was a really good time until we got back to Vinny's place and saw what had taken place," said Lizzy with pride.

"Lizzy and I are old friends, and we hung out yesterday for the first time in ages," I said to Lola, looking into her eyes.

"Sounds like fun," Lola said somewhat sarcastically.

"Look, it doesn't matter what happened yesterday besides this 'break-in' we both experienced. Our landlord is going to fucking kill us!" I said, trying to steer the conversation back to where it should be.

"Oh, right! I forgot to mention that," replied Lola. "She came by last night right after the ambulance took you away, and boy oh boy, she wasn't too happy. She said you're going to have to pay half the amount for the damage caused since you forgot to lock the door."

"Oh, that's fucking bullshit! Are you kidding me?!" I replied in anger and disbelief.

"Yes, sir," Lola said.

"Fuck that bitch. She can take a one-way trip to fuck-off island!" I said, feeling very frustrated.

"Yeah. I'm really sorry about this, Vincent," said Lola.

I didn't really know what to say back to her. The fact that I have to pay for half the damage that I didn't even caused or want caused really got to me. I felt like calling my landlord and bitching the shit out of her. Like seriously, this is so not fair and I'm the victim here. Why does a current victim have to be further victimized? Straight horse manure, if you ask me.

"So on a scale of one to ten, how hungover are you?" Liz asked me with a half smile on her face.

"Seven. How about you?" I replied to her.

"I'm a solid eight, I'd say," she said, laughing a bit.

"So," Lola interrupted, "how much longer do you have to be here for?"

"Well, the nurse and doctors said that I'm going to at least have to spend the rest of the day here and get to leave the following morning," I replied to her.

"Is there anything I can get for you while you stay here?" she asked me politely.

"No. I think I'll be able to survive. I would like to go outside for a cigarette though to be perfectly honest," I said.

"Let's see if the doctors can allow you out!" said Liz.

"Oh, they can. I just have to be on psych ward property," I said to the girls.

"Okay, let's go then," said Lola.

The two girls managed to find my doctor and ask if it was okay for me to go out for a smoke with them. The three of them then came back into my room, and the doctor said it was okay but after the smoke, the girls would have to leave since visiting time was close to the end. The three of us then all proceeded outside, and both Lo and Liz gave me a cigarette each. We all lit up our smokes and sat on a bench far away from the wild ones but still on hospital property.

"What are your plans for the rest of the day when we leave?" Lola asked me.

"Probably not much. I mean, in a way, this is almost the only place I have left," I said as I hung my head low.

"Aw, Vincent it'll be okay! I'll swing by and I can help you clean your place up!" said Lizzy very cheerfully.

"Thanks, Liz," I replied to her softly.

"And I live in the same house as you so I can also help!" Lola mentioned politely.

"Yeah, we'll have a group cleanup!" said Lizzy.

"Thanks, guys, I really appreciate it!" I said to them.

We finished our cigarettes, and the girls said their good-byes to me as they hopped in Lizzy's car and took off. Sitting at the bench all alone while lighting a smoke, I had a big realization in my head. I don't have to do this anymore if I don't want to. And I don't want to. What do I have to live for anyways? Absolutely nothing! Those dreams/visions of my family were more than enough for me to become very comfortable with the idea of committing suicide myself. I mean, at least I'll be with my family whether they're in heaven or hell or even oblivion. As long as I'm with them, I don't give a fuck. So just like that, I started thinking of a suicide plan for myself, and I was starting to become very excited about it! I'm going to see my parents again! Now I really can't wait to get out of here. I forgot to check my mattress in my bedroom during the night of the break in, but I did notice that it wasn't ransacked or moved around at all, which meant my father's ten-gauge shotgun was still inside of my mattress. Sweet! Not only am I going to die the exact same way my biggest idol did (Kurt Cobain), I'm also going to go out with a bang and get to see my family! I mean, they were all telling me to join them and that's all I truly want. I didn't even ask to be born, never mind living the shittiest life imaginable, so why not? I started becoming very fascinated and excited with the idea, and on top of that, I didn't have to worry about writing a suicide note either because I don't have anyone in my life anyways.

"Okay, guys, it's lunchtime! Everyone back inside, please!" yelled a sexy-looking nurse as she walked outside to inform all the nutjobs.

Fuck yeah, it's already lunch! Time is flying by quickly, and I'm starting to become more relieved and content about the decision I had made. I went inside with all the other schizophrenics and went back into my room where I waited for a nurse to bring me my lunch. A nurse eventually made her way into my room and dropped off a platter with my lunch on it: two slices of pizza, rice pudding, a small salad, and chicken noodle soup. Not a bad lunch for a psych ward. I finished my lunch quickly and then decided to go into the chill spot/lobby and see if they have a copy of *Catcher in the Rye* because that's my favorite book of all time, and since I'm ending my life tomorrow, I might as well live it up a bit before dying. Maybe they have my favourite movie, *Casablanca*. What would the odds be if both were there? Probably one in a couple hundred thousand at least. It felt kind of weird walking through the ward to the main chill area. I don't consider myself to be as far gone as these other locos in here, but at the time, I asked myself, "Okay, why are *you* in here then?" All I can think of is my blackouts. I was doing fine for a long while, but then Lola entered into my life, and now I've had a few in less than a week…I truly believe it's because I care about her, and people I care about, I love. Not like romantically per se, but just genuinely give a fuck about. Before Lola, I was having blackouts because I lost my mom. It started off as a daily thing but became less aggressive in nature and way more spaced out. I went about five to six months without one, and that was a record time too! Then Lo came along. I mean, she was always there in a way, but not like the way she has been lately. Having fun with Lizzy was fantastic, to say the least, but boy, I can't begin to imagine how hot sex would be with Lo. Oh my goodness!

Finally making it to the lobby, you're not going to believe what I found—*Catcher in the Rye*! I was mind blown that at least one of these was actually there, but I couldn't shake what I was just thinking of: Lola. I wanted to leave the psych ward then and there just so I could run back to the duplex, run up her stairs to her place, grab her, and passionately kiss her. The thought of actually going ahead and doing that didn't seem too crazy to me. I mean, she was the one who threw me on my bed and got on top of me…Wait a minute, I got it! Before I end my life so I could be with my family, I'll take Lola on a date! We'll get fucked up, go to dinner, maybe a movie after, and then hot sex afterward! This is all too good. And it starts off by me taking this goldmine of a book back into my room and reading it! Wow, I'm really happy right now. I mean, I wish I didn't have to kill myself, but I know those dreams were more than just dreams. They felt way too real not to be. As I was walking through the psych ward to my room, some guy passed me in the hallway and then turned around.

"Hey, Vincent. I'm Chad," said Chad, a person who I've never met before.

"Umm, hello there. How do you know my name?" I asked this Chad character.

"Oh, she told me your name," he replied.

"Who told you my name?" I asked him.

"The witch," he responded.

"Excuse me? What the fuck are you talking about, bro?" I asked him, feeling caught off guard and puzzled.

"She was here today. I know it. I could feel it," he said, looking afraid.

"Who are you talking about, dude?" I asked Chad.

"Come, sit with me at this table, and we'll get into detail," he said as he pointed to an empty table.

"Lead the way," I said.

"Okay, so you're in danger. You know that?" he asked me very shortly after we sat down.

"From who? Who the fuck is this witch that you speak of?" I asked him, thinking that this guy is so far gone, he's seeing witches in the psych ward!

"She was in your dreams, and she has you wrapped around her finger. The more time you spend with her, the more power you bring her," he said to me in a very poetic fashion. This guy is definitely bonkers.

"Are you talking about Lola?!" I asked him in surprise, considering he knew what my dream was about!

"*She's a witch! Kill her! Kill her now while you still can*!" he screamed at the top of lungs as his pupils dilated and his skin got pale.

Three security guards came by really quick to subdue him and then take him away. I know what just happened. I just talked to Lola's boyfriend. And it was really scary.

Chapter 11

I can't believe that just happened. How the fuck did Chad know that Lola was in my dreams and not only that, but that she was evil too. This is all bullshit to me. I just can't buy it, you know. Lola really being a witch? I thought witches only came out at night and were mostly spotted over in the Middle East and India. Witches are supposed to be old as fuck too—long ass noses, wrinkly skin, blueish-greenish face, and they're supposed to fly on brooms too, which is something I've never seen Lola do before. I'm just going to go to my room and read my favorite book.

On my way there, I bumped into one of my favorite doctors! Dr. Leonard. She was a beautiful doctor, extremely caring and nice, plus she looked like a blonde babe straight out of the nineties—long blond hair; literally perfect body; massive ass and titties; gorgeous face; and very mean, sexy-looking eyes. She was the doctor that looked after me when I had to stay here because my mother died. She took so much care of me. She always reassured me that everything would be okay, and she even used to hook me up with Xanax instead of lorazepam, which was fucking awesome!

"Oh my! Vincent, is that you?" Dr. Leonard asked me.

"Yes, it is, Dr. Leonard," I replied with a smile on my face.

"Oh my goodness. What happened to your head, sweetie?" she asked me, genuinely looking concerned.

"It's a long story, to be honest. I blacked out after my place was smashed up and broken into and I fell down my front steps," I explained to her.

"Your place got broken into? Vincent, I'm so sorry!" she said. "Can I give you a hug?"

"I would love a hug! I missed you, Dr. Leonard," I admitted to her.

"You're such a sweetie, you know that, Vincent?" she asked me as she gave me a big, warm hug.

"I really missed you," I said again to her, knowing that it might possibly sound weird, but oh well.

I almost started crying on her shoulder as she gave me that warm hug. It brought back a feeling of nostalgia but in a depressing way. It reminded me of my mother dying. I could tell that she knew how I was feeling and decided to walk me back to my room. We talked on the way there and even had a few laughs.

"Hey, Doctor, I was wondering, you wouldn't be able to slip me a Xan or two, would you?" I asked, feeling a little bit of desperation just at the thought of it.

"You know it, pumpkin," she replied, winking her left eye at me.

"You're the best, you know that?" I asked her.

"Oh, believe me, I know that, Vinny," she said, cracking a wide, beautiful smile. Her teeth were so perfect and white!

"Ha ha ha ha!" I laughed as I sat on my bed and made tower of pillows to rest my head on while I read.

"I'll be back very soon with that snack for you. Sound good, champ?" she asked me.

"Almost sounds too good to be true to be perfectly honest," I stated back to her.

She smiled and then walked out of my room, slowly and quietly closing the door. I decided to lie down and crack into my book. I've read this book probably twenty-five to thirty times in my whole life, so I'm at the point where I can just scan through the pages without having to read every word but still knowing every detail of the story. I love this book so much because when I read it for the first time, I literally thought it was written about me! I thought that I was Holden Caufield. His character and personality matched mine so damn perfect that it was almost scary. Right before I opened the book, Dr. Leonard returned to my room and she had a small paper cup with a 1mg blue oval Xanax. The blue ones are the best ones too!

"Thank you so much, Dr. Leonard!" I said to the beautiful doctor who had just gone out of her way to get me Xanax. God, I love this doctor.

"I'll be back later on to check on you, okay, Vin?" she asked me ever so politely.

"Please do, it was so nice finally getting to see you again!" I said as the Xanax kicked in, considering I just chewed it instead of swallowing it.

"Okay, enjoy your book, Vincent. I shall return later on," she said to me again.

"Thank you," I said one final time before she left my room.

Damn, I felt amazing! I haven't had Xanax in quite a while, and man, I got me high as a kite! I felt extremely comfortable lying down in my bed with that mountain of pillows my head was resting on. I opened up my book and finally started reading it. I read through about the first forty-five pages, and just like that, I was starting to nod off. Eventually, I fell asleep. And as usual, more dreams about Lola. Except these were different…dreams of her and I on a beautiful island together, lying on the beach, and soaking up some sun; some dreams about me and her hanging out in the woods on a cliff, watching the sunset and kissing one another. It was so profound. I even had a few dreams of her and me fucking. I mean, I don't remember much but know for fact that that's what had occurred considering how hard my dick was when I finally woke up. It was about three and a half hours that I had a nap, and I felt really good. I woke up feeling completely in love and happy. I couldn't wait to leave this place so I could see Lola again. I miss her. I sat there in my bed thinking about the sweet dreams I had just experienced, and before I knew it, Dr. Leonard came back into my room.

"Morning, sunshine!" she said to me with her pretty voice that lit up the entire room.

"Why, hello there, gorgeous," I replied to her in a very slick manner.

"How was your nap? I came by earlier but saw that you were out like a light, so I didn't want to wake you up," she explained to me.

"Why, thank you for that! And it was very good, thank you for asking," I replied.

"I'm glad to hear that, Vincent," she said with a smile on her face. "How is your head feeling?"

"It honestly doesn't feel bad at all. I haven't had Advil or Tylenol in a very long time, and it hasn't been bothering me at all," I said to the doctor.

"Okay, that's a very good sign! That means your minor concussion is healing already," she explained to me.

"Yeah. Anyways, Dr. Leonard, I was wondering if I could ask you something?" I asked her hesitantly.

"Shoot for the stars, Vinny," she answered back.

"What's your opinion on suicide? I know I've asked this before, but seriously, what if my family is currently wanting me to kill myself so I could be with them?" I fired away.

"Where did you come up with a crazy idea like that, Vince?" she asked me, looking concerned.

"I had a dream about my family, and they all told me to kill myself so I could be with them and no longer have to suffer," I revealed to her.

"Oh, Vincent. I'm so sorry. Suicide is a result of suffering however. It wouldn't make sense for your family to want you to suffer in order to be with them. They love you too much for that, Vincent. They want to see you prosper in life and not have the same fate they had. Besides, you think I didn't see you with your girlfriend and her friend this afternoon?" she said to me.

"That's very funny and kind of you, but I haven't dated Lizzy for years now," I responded.

"Is she the blonde one?" she asked.

"Yeah, why?" I asked her.

"No, I was talking about the other one. The one with the black hair! She was checking you out like crazy," she elaborated.

Holy damn! Lola was checking me out? Oh, my god! That's fantastic news! I can't believe it. Holy shit, I'm so happy right now. Lola likes me! Yes! Score 1 for Vinny!

"Oh yeah. No, she's not my girlfriend. I wish though," I replied.

"I think she's only a question away from being your girlfriend, Vincent. Believe me on this one," said Dr. Leonard.

"Thanks for letting me know that, Dr. Leonard! You're the best!" I reminded her again.

Dr. Leonard stayed with me for a bit, and we talked about life and other random subjects. She left me alone in my room eventually, and I decided to read my book a little more. I ended up crushing about forty pages in less than half an hour before I got bored of reading and wanted to do something else. For some reason, I started thinking of Lola's ex-boyfriend and all of that fucked-up shit he told me about. I didn't believe it though. I think he was beyond crazy to think such things about such a beauty like Lola. Maybe he was jealous because she told him about me or something. Who knows! All I know is that tomorrow morning I'll be checking out of this place and her ex probably won't leave anytime soon considering how he acted today. Dinner was eventually served at the ward, and just like that, it was evening time and the sun had already gone down. I was feeling very excited about actually being able to leave and then going on a date with Lola! There's no way that she's going to say no. All I need to do is get one passionate kiss in, and the rest will be smooth sailing. Dinner wasn't all too bad that evening: meat loaf with mashed potatoes and coleslaw; cheesecake for dessert with vanilla ice cream on the side. I swear every time I come back here to the psych ward, the food just gets better and better. It's almost tempting to want to stay longer than you're welcome because I have nothing to go back to when I'm out of here other than my completely smashed-up duplex.

I was in my room reading my book when a doctor with a nurse came in. This time it was Dr. Hansen and Nurse McHam.

"Hello, Vincent. We're here to ask you a few simple questions before we get you ready for your discharge tomorrow, all right?" asked the doctor.

"Sounds good to me," I replied to him.

"First off, how is your head feeling?" he asked me.

"Not bad. On and off pain but it's very mild," I answered.

"Okay, that's very good to hear!" he stated.

"We know about what happened to your place, and we're very sorry, Vincent. Are you going to be okay going back to your duplex?" asked the nurse.

"I guess I don't really have a choice, do I?" I stated.

"Well, no. We do offer emergency housing if someone really requires it," she answered.

"No, I think I'll be okay to go back," I said, thinking about Lola.

"Are you sure?" asked the doctor.

"One hundred percent, Doc," I said.

"Okay, so, we're going to give you a prescription for Invega that you will have to take once a month, but other than that, we urge you to stay on your methadone and clozapine, okay?" explained the doctor.

"I don't have a problem with that at all. Anything else that I need to do?" I asked.

"Yes, we think it would be wise if you could pick up some Tylenol and Advil for yourself in case you start getting some headaches," stated the nurse.

"Sounds good," I replied calmly.

"Okay, Vincent. We'll be back with a dose of lorazepam, and then it's time for bed," said the doctor as he got up with the nurse, and they both left the room.

"Awesome, thank you!" I said as the door shut behind them.

Very interesting, I feel genuinely happy. I'm not sure if whether it's from the fact that I'm going to get to plow Lola before I blow my brains out or the aftermath: me seeing my parents again, except this time, staying with them! The doctors and nurses didn't suspect a thing either. They thought I was being hopeful and honest about wanting to get back to my completely destroyed place and start cleaning up as if nothing happened. I was playing it perfectly! They ain't got shit on me. I waited in my bed patiently for the doctor and/or nurse to come back and even tried to meditate for a couple of minutes. I was in a very deep state when the sound of the door opening distracted me and drew all my focus away from my breath, resulting in an abrupt ending to a very nice meditation. I opened my eyes and saw that only the nurse had returned.

"Welcome back," I decided to greet her with.

"Long time no see, hey?" she replied in a comic manner.

"Too long, much, much too long if you ask me," I said with a grin on my face.

"Ha ha ha. Okay, here's your lorazepam and a cup of water to drink before dissolving the tablet, all right?" she stated to me.

"Sounds like a plan to me!" I replied.

She handed me both cups, and I drank the water quickly and then grabbed the 2mg tablet and stuck it right underneath my tongue. They're so nice to me here at the psych ward. They've been getting my methadone delivered here for me because they know that I'm prescribed to it for opiate replacement therapy reasons.

"I hope you have a great sleep, Vincent, and tomorrow around ten to ten thirty a.m. will be the time you should be able to leave at. Might be a little before or a little after, but around that time. We'll have a doctor and nurse come in the room to check on you, and judging how that goes, you'll know whether you can leave earlier in the day or later on, okay?" the nurse explained to me.

"I like the sounds of that, not going to lie," I replied to her with a grin.

"Okay, great! I hope you have a great sleep, Vincent. Good night!" she said to me with a pretty smile on her face.

"Thanks! I hope the rest of your shift goes well," I said, smiling back.

"Thank you! That's very kind," she replied as she left the room.

I sat up in bed thinking of how good of a day I just had and kept thinking of Lola. Maybe she could be the one to save me from myself. I mean, how is she going to feel when she finds my dead body with the whole face missing? And what about Lizzy? Maybe she didn't come over randomly that day, maybe it was the universe trying to get us back together. Is that really it though? Will having a girlfriend be a good idea or just a shit load of emotional stress and scarring? Having borderline personality disorder, relationships tend to be very rocky, unpredictable, and, overall, very stressful and dramatic in the end. Or maybe enough time has passed, and my symptoms have subsided at least a little bit. I guess I'll never know until I try. So fuck it, why not? If it doesn't work out, then perhaps it was never meant to be, and maybe Lizzy is the one who will give me a reason to stay on this lonesome planet. Those dreams or visions or whatever may have been convincing, but how do I know they weren't cloaked? Like what if my family members were demons in disguise trying to get me to kill myself instead of living out the rest of my life? If that was the case, why was it a demonic version of Lola that was pulling me away from the ones I love and miss the most? I wish I had answers to all of these questions, but maybe one day I will. I made myself very comfortable in my bed and decided to red some more of my favorite book. I've been reading this for less than a day, and I'm well over 50 percent finished already! And just like that, before I even knew it, I fell asleep.

I woke up inside my house and heard a noise coming from the living room. As soon as I entered the room, I saw my mother, father, and older sister waiting inside for me to come in so they could yell "*Surprise*" and then proceed to singing me Happy Birthday. I remembered this moment, and as strange as this may sound, I felt déjà vu in my dream… I was either four or five years old in the dream, but somehow I was the same height as I am in reality and I could talk. I guess they saw me as a young boy. I sat at the seat they reserved for me, and we had cake.

Chapter 12

We sat there eating my birthday cake and laughing about old memories. It was beyond incredible to be with them again, especially since it felt so genuine. It wasn't even a lucid dream either. It was just me in a very happy dream with the people I love the most. Eventually, all good things must come to an end. And that's exactly what happened with this heavenly like dream I was having that night. It eventually did become a lucid dream! I remember all of a sudden having the realization that this was a memory that had already occurred, and since I know it's impossible to recreate past memories in reality, this was a dream! The only problem with waking up inside your dream is that everyone that is in your dream starts disappearing and vanishing until you're the only one left. Just like that, I was all alone in the living room. I looked to the right where my kitchen was, and there was no one in there, so I decided to go outside, to my backyard, and go in the garage where I found my sister's smashed-up car with her dead body inside of it. Scared as all hell, I ran out of the garage only to see my mom standing on the roof of the house, waving good-bye to me. I screamed, *"No!"* at the top of my lungs, but it didn't stop her from making herself fall off the roof and right through the ground below. I looked over to my right, and there was my dad sitting on one of the chairs in the backyard polishing his shotgun while looking at me and smiling. I tried to scream and tell him to put his gun down, but instead, he just put the double barrel into his mouth and hit the trigger. The sound of the shotgun blast was enough to completely change the environment of the dream from a beautiful sunny-filled day to a dark, creepy dungeon. I was tied up and strapped down to some wooden table. There were satanic symbols all over the walls and on the floor with candles as well. Soon enough, some scary-looking Satanists entered the room I was in and started practicing a ritual. A ritual that summoned a demon right from the ground within the pentagram! It was a horribly disfigured-looking female demon with contorting arms and legs along with a sleek black liquid dripping off her body. The Satanists kept rehearsing the same mantra while staying in their positions while the demonic abomination started walking closer and closer to me. I tried screaming and moving, but I couldn't. This was a fucking horrible nightmare! Soon enough, the disgusting humanoid ghoul was right in front of me, and it started licking my face with its extremely long, snakelike tongue. The mantra being repeated by the satanic bastards got louder and louder. The demon undid my pants, pull them down along with my underwear, and laughed at my small penis. She then grabbed it with her left hand and squeezed it very hard. She held it with her left hand while slowly inserting her right hand's pointer finger directly into my dickhole! The pain was that of nothing I've ever felt before! I tried screaming so hard, but nothing was coming, and this demonic bitch started squeezing her middle finger in as well! I looked down and could see that my dick was starting to bleed, but that didn't stop the demon from doing her best to finger blast my peehole. I closed my eyes and tried to shake myself around and hopefully wake up in another dream. A much less sinister one would be preferred! And it worked! Only problem was, it was only my mind that was awake… I woke up in my room at the psych ward in a state of sleep paralysis with that ugly bitch-ass demon sitting on my chest, watching me as I hopelessly try to break free from the paralysis. I closed my eyes and tried so hard to get my arms and legs to move, and finally, it actually happened! I was free! I opened my eyes to see that the demon was gone and that I wasn't in a secondary state of sleep paralysis.

I sat up in my bed, absolutely covered in sweat, thinking about the horrible dreams I just had. There was a box of Kleenex on the night table beside my bed, so I grabbed a few tissues and wiped off my face. I couldn't believe how fucked up those dreams were! Like seriously, it started off as one of the greatest dreams I've ever had in my life, but then somehow being one of the worst night terrors I've ever experienced before! Then I heard someone from the outside of my room come up to my door and opened it. It was a doctor with two security guards.

"Whoa, what's going on here, fellas?" I asked the three of them.

"I was going to ask you the exact same thing, Vincent. What's going on here?" the doctor asked me.

"What exactly are you talking about here, Doc?" I asked him.

"Why are you awake and screaming at the top of your lungs, Vincent?" he asked me with a concerned look on his face.

"I wasn't screaming, and I'm awake because I just had a horrific nightmare followed by sleep paralysis," I explained to him.

"Okay. Well, there was a lot of screaming coming from your room, so we thought we'd check up to make sure everything's okay," he stated.

"Well, I was trying to scream during this nightmare and paralysis, so maybe I was screaming in real life but not the dream," I reasoned.

"All right. Well, it looks like everything is okay over here for now, but if we hear anymore screaming from you, we're going to have to give you something to help you sleep and possible undergo some tests, okay?" the doctor said to me.

"Sure, sounds good. Thank you, guys!" I said to them as they all turned away simultaneously and headed for the door.

I don't know if I'm going to be able to fall asleep again after that. It felt so real, and the pain was absolutely unbearable! I then remembered that your chances of sleep paralysis are lessened if you sleep on one of your sides. So I decided to turn and face the white wall and hopefully fall asleep without having to go through hell again in order to wake up. Anyways, I ended up falling asleep, and this time, it was a good one! It was about Lola. She and I were sitting underneath a tree in some beautiful landscape just staring at the clouds, and we were both eating apples. Almost as if we were symbolizing Adam and Eve in a way. Either way, we were having a great time! We were both laughing and joking around like crazy, and animals were approaching us and didn't seem frightened of us at all. Squirrels, birds, rabbits, deer, mice, and even some geese! It was a beautiful sight to behold, to say the least, and it felt like everything was perfect. Until there was a sound, like a big bang or a thunderous roar, that sounded like it came from very far away but it was so loud, every and anything could hear its presence. The skies became dark gray, and the beautiful animals all ran away. A heavy wind picked up, and just like that, the dream was ruined. And not only that, there was something there with us, some kind of entity.

Lola latched on to me and buried her head in my chest, not wanting to look at what might be coming right at us. I don't blame her. It was some creepy-looking demon staring me right in my eyes. It was a male demon and looked horrifying. And not only that, he has an absolutely massive penis! This creature was about ten to eleven feet tall, and its penis went down to its knee. So in other words, it was as long as my arm! It was bigger than any dildo I've even seen in sex shops when Lizzy used to take me when we had relations for quite some time. This demon looked like a Greek or Roman god or something. His body was so fucking ripped, and he was at least twice the size of Arnold Schwarzenegger. He towered over Lola and me and just kept staring deep into my eyes. He stood there long enough to clearly make me realize that not only was he bigger than me, he was an evil entity of some sort, literally straight out of hell. He looked tormented and had very wrinkled, pale white skin with completely red-and-black eyes, teeth of a wolf, horns of a goat, massive pair of bat wings on his back, and even the tail he had was a snake! It had goat legs, that massive thunder cock, the tongue of a lizard, and, honestly, he kind of looked like Baphomet.

"Rise!" he commanded me.

I was so fucking terrified my whole entire body was shaking! I looked down and saw Lola was no longer there anymore. It was just me, sitting underneath this tree now. Even as scared as I was, I decided to do what the ghoul demanded and stoop up. He was so tall, that my face was literally only up to his dick…which was fucking huge!

"Who in the fuck are you?" I somehow managed to ask the terrifying beast.

"Diabolus, and your soul is mine!" he responded with a haunting laugh afterward.

"Why are you trying to take my soul? I know you can't because I believe in God, and he can destroy you in the snap of a finger!" I told the demon.

"God could never save you. It's too late, you fool!" he said to me.

"It's never too late, mother fucker!" I yelled at him in anger.

Just like that, I was lifted into the air by the demon simply by him using his right hand to effortlessly lift me up in midair. He lifted me high enough so that we were face-to-face, staring one another right in the eyes.

"You think you're a funny guy?" asked Diabolus.

"Yes, I do. And on top of that, I think you're a funny-looking guy!" I yelled at his face.

He lifted his right hand up, and I went flying back, slamming against the tree I was once peacefully sitting under with Lola until the demonic shithead came by and ruined everything! It hurt quite a bit, and I was pinned against the tree as if I was stapled to it in a way.

"Well, you're not going to be laughing when you openhandedly give me your soul, you little fuck!" the demon yelled at me. "You're going to suffer for eternity!" He started laughing very loudly and maniacally.

All of a sudden, I was free from the force of the demon, falling down immediately and hitting the grass pretty hard. I remember looking up and the demon was no longer there anymore. The landscape environment I was in was all collapsing and folding in on itself. The dream was finally coming to an end, and before I knew it, I woke up in my room at the psych ward. I woke up feeling good however, which for me, is extremely rare. I felt like I had one of the best sleeps of my whole entire life, and I felt really energized. I sat up in my bed, and I wasn't even tired at all. It was a miracle, if you ask me!

A very short while later, as expected, a doctor and a nurse both came inside my room.

"Good morning, Vincent! How did you sleep?" the doctor asked very enthusiastically.

"Honestly, really good," I replied to him.

That's good to hear! Nothing like a good night's rest. Anyways, how is your head feeling, Vincent?" he asked me.

"I feel no pain whatsoever," I told him.

"How are you feeling physically, Vincent?" asked the nurse.

"I feel really good actually. I feel like I have a lot of energy, and I'm also in a surprisingly good mood as well," I said to her.

"Okay, good to hear! We're just going to test your vitals, and after that, a nurse will come by to drop off your breakfast," the doctor then explained to me.

"Sounds good to me, Doc!" I stated.

They checked my vitals, and everything was normal. They did a few more tests, but they were really quick. Shortly after the nurse and doctor had left, another nurse came into my room.

"Hi, there. I'm Kelly, and I'm a nurse here. I just wanted to ask…first of all, you're Vincent, correct?" she asked me.

"Why, yes. Yes, I am Vincent indeed," I replied with a very sophisticated tone, which made her laugh harder than I thought it would.

"Wonderful accent, I must say. Anyways, I wanted to ask. Did you want to take your medication before or after breakfast?" she asked kindly.

"I'll take it afterward," I answered.

"Okay, and that's just your regular dose of methadone and 15mg Diazepam, correct?" she asked.

"Yes. However, if you could provide me with two blues, that would be very kind of you," I said with a grin on my face as I was trying to bribe her into giving me a little more Valium than usual.

"That's no problem at all! Is there anything else I can get for you before I grab your breakfast?" she asked me very kindly.

"Just breakfast and then medication, sweetie. Thank you so much for being so kind," I said to her.

"It's my job, Vincent. I love taking care of people!" she said as she smiled.

"Awesome," I stated.

She came back into my room less than a minute after leaving to grab my breakfast for me. She gave the tray along with my medications on another platter, which she placed by my bedside table.

"Enjoy your breakfast, Vincent! The doctor and nurse should return within the next forty-five minutes or so, and they will let you know what time you can leave today, all right?" the nurse explained ever so nicely.

"Sounds like a great idea to me, Kelly. Thanks again for being so awesome!" I said to her, smiling.

She left the room, and I immediately checked one of the cups on the tray of my medications to see if she had actually brought me two Valiums, but no, she gave me three instead! Damn, what an incredible nurse! The breakfast I had was also absolutely delicious! French toast with scrambled eggs and bacon! Alongside some sausages and a little bowl of Cheerios too! I crushed the whole breakfast in less than five minutes. I was so hungry and feeling so good that I put that shit away no problem! I then took my medications, placed the breakfast tray on the night table, and decided to read my book until the doctor and nurse come back. Eventually, a good twenty minutes had passed and Kelly swung by to pick up my breakfast and medication trays. About five to six minutes after that, the doctor and nurse came back to my room.

"All right, Vincent. We got all your test results, and we don't have a reason to keep you here any longer. If you wish, you can stay for an additional three hours, but after that, you will need to exit the property," he said to me.

"Awesome! That's great news! I'm not going to lie, I'm probably going to head out right away then," I revealed to them.

"Sounds good, Vincent! Is there anything else we can do for you before you leave?" the nurse asked me.

"No, I think I should be just fine. Thank you," I replied to her.

"All right then, Vincent. We'll let you get ready to go," said the nurse.

I didn't really have a lot of stuff with me at all. All I had was the clothing I wore that night, my wallet, phone, and my pack of smokes. I quickly changed outfits and got everything sorted out. I stepped out of the room and saw a security guard very nearby.

"Hey, are you Vincent?" he asked me in his thick African tone.

"Yeah, why?" I asked the big fella.

"I'm the security guard who's in charge of walking you out of the ward," he explained.

"Okay, awesome! Let's go," I said to him.

He walked me to the reception area/front entrance to the ward. As I made my way out, three different nurses said good-bye to me and that made me feel like a fucking pimp!

"All right, buddy. I hope everything goes well for you. God bless," said the security guard.

"Thanks, dude. You have a great day!" I said as I walked out of the psych ward and immediately lit up a cigarette.

I started walking home at a normal walking pace because I knew what kind of state my duplex was in. I felt beyond depressed and didn't really think of a plan as to what to do when I get there. But then I remembered it all! If Lola ends up becoming my girlfriend, then I'll be the happiest man alive. If not, then I'll just kill myself and finally get to be with my family again. A smile then formed on my face as I literally just realized that either way, I'm going to die very happy. I was almost at home and debating whether or not I should write a suicide note. To who though?

Lola, Lizzy, and that's it? That's bullshit, fuck a suicide note! If my family was around, I'd include them, but then again, I wouldn't want to commit suicide if I had my whole family together with me. I guess that was a pretty stupid thought…

Anyways, it was pretty cold outside, and I felt sad knowing what I was going to come home to. I finally made it home through the freezing autumn wind and walked up to the front door. I couldn't actually remember if I even locked the place when Lizzy and I came back from our date. I decided to try opening the door without using the keys, and boom! the door was unlocked and flew wide open. No surprise there. It was freezing inside too because some of the windows had been smashed. There was red-and- black spray paint all over the walls, some of which displayed satanic symbolism. Maybe those creepy ass freaks from the cemetery that Lola and I were at did this! But I just can't understand how nobody seems to know a thing about who did it. Apparently, no witnesses, nothing! Fucking horseshit! There was something that didn't feel right about my place. Not just because it was trashed and shit, but a strange energy/vibration was now occupying the place. I felt as if whoever did this, must of casted a spell either during or just after trashing the place and leaving, therefore making me think that it actually really was those weird cult cocksuckers. I walked into my bedroom, and thankfully, the window in there wasn't smashed, but the whole place was still a wreck. I didn't even bother looking around. I just pulled the curtains and blinds shut and turned on the lamp after I picked it up from the floor. I lifted up my mattress, and there it was, my daddy's beautiful shotgun. Cleaned, restored, locked and loaded, baby! I picked it up and decided to sit on my bed while examining the firearm. Thinking about the fact that this shotgun took my father's life, and that tonight, it may or may not take mine. I decided to look directly down the barrel with both eyes while lightly holding my finger on the trigger. I wonder where I'd go if I decided to just do it then and there. As usual though, the thought of lonely old Lola hearing the news or seeing the scene and becoming depressed came. I mean, I'm still not actually 100 percent about Lola liking me back equally as much as I like her, I mean, love. I can't believe I'm saying it this early, but I'm in love with Lola. I got to admit it, she has me wrapped around her finger. Also, as usual, just when I was thinking about her and remembering the date we had, I heard a knock on my front door. I could genuinely feel her presence close to me as I walked toward the front door to unlock it and open it. I opened it to see Lo starting there in a very cute burgundy parka with a matching color toque.

"Oh hey!" I said as I pretended as if I wasn't expecting anyone to come visit me at my trashed place.

"Hey, munchkin!" said Lola as she came in and gave me a big hug.

"What's the good word?" I asked her, feeling so happy that she had decided to come see me. She smelled so good too!

"I just wanted to see how you're doing! I heard you come into the house, so I figured I'd check up on you," she said to me politely.

"Well, isn't that sweet of you!" I told her.

"Yeah, I was going to ask if you needed help with anything like cleaning or borrowing money or just to have someone around to talk to," she nicely offered.

"That's very kind of you, Lo. I actually do need you for something now that I think of it," I said to her.

"Shoot!" she replied.

"I want to go out on a date tonight, but I have no one who wants to come with me," I explained to her.

"Oh no! What about Lizzy or whatever her name is," she replied in an odd tone.

"Nope, not even her," I said while purposely making a sad face.

"Well, it looks like you won't be alone after all since I have no plans at all tonight," she said, grinning at me.

"Oh my god! Thank you, Jesus!" I said.

"Oh, shush!" she stated.

"Is there anything particular that you would like to do tonight? Dinner and a movie?" I mentioned to her.

"I think that sounds like a great time, Vincent! Let's do dinner and a movie," she answered.

"Awesome, what do you have planned before then?" I asked her.

"I have to go out and get a couple things," she responded.

"All right, well, I'll be here. Going through all of this trash and probably not accomplishing much," I said in a disappointed tone.

"Oh, I won't be long. I'm getting picked up by my friend at 7-Eleven, so I should be back in the next hour! I'll help you out for a bit, and then we can go out!" she said cheerfully, obviously trying to make me feel better, which 100 percent worked by the way.

"Okay, sweet! I'll be waiting for you then," I said, staring into her eyes.

"See you soon, Vinny," she said with a grin, staring back into my eyes, damn!

She walked away from the duplex looking ever so beautiful while doing so. I can't imagine the amount of looks from guys she gets on a daily basis, both online and in physical reality. Probably fifty to one hundred minimum. I stayed outside watching her walking down the sidewalk until I couldn't see her before going back inside. I decided to go into my kitchen to see if I could make a cup of tea. Believe it or not, there were actually some glasses that weren't smashed, and they didn't take any of my teas! I guess it's true when it is said to enjoy the little things in life! My kettle wasn't damaged at all either, so I got the water ready to boil and then went into my bedroom where I decided to hide the shotgun back under my mattress. I figured I'd just lie down in my bed and wait for the water to finishing boiling before getting up again. I lay there thinking about lots of things: my upcoming date with Lola, those intense dreams I had, and the fact that my placed had been trashed. What a crazy last week it's been. I really hope that Lola is into me. I swear, she's hands down and arguably the most beautiful chick I've ever seen in my life. I just kept imagining how amazing it would be even just to make out with her. Such a pretty face, mystical eyes, perfect teeth and smile. Her body was another story. Long story short, it was perfect. She was everything I could possibly want in a dream girl. Not just the whole emo/scene look either, I like everything about her! Her voice, her laugh, her interest in the occult, the fact that she plays guitar and skates too. God, I hope she likes me! The kettle finally finished boiling, so I got up and made my way into the kitchen.

Chapter 13

I decided to make myself a green tea with some honey in it. I had a massive feeling of depression on my chest, which came out of nowhere. Probably had to do with the fact that my whole entire placed was destroyed and that somehow I'd have to fix it up in time before cold-ass winter comes along. And along with seasonal change, comes seasonable depression. Doesn't my life sound fantastic? Anyways, I ended up going outside with my green tea in hand to enjoy a cigarette on my front steps. I knew that I should be cleaning up instead of just fucking around, but what does it matter anyways? This place is going to be even more of a mess when my blood and brains soak the white walls in a nice dark-red concoction. I thought about what my final words should be or if I should do something crazy like blow my brains out at church during a Sunday morning service. I guess it would be more of a Sunday "mourning" service… Fuck, that's dark!

I started cleaning up and organizing everything into two piles: one for stuff in good enough condition to keep and the other pile for stuff destroyed beyond belief. It was very heartbreaking going through all of this stuff that used to be in perfect placement and perfect condition. It was also very angering as well. I literally would probably kill the fuckers who did this if I ever found out somehow. The pile with stuff completely destroyed stuff was way bigger than my "keepers" pile, and that shattered my heart even more. Pictures of my mom and dad in smashed picture frames and with the actual pictures being ripped and torn too. Eventually, it was just too much for me. I couldn't look at all of this stuff anymore, and I was started feeling irritated about the fact that Lola hasn't come back yet. Like what the fuck! Either way, I decided it would be a good idea to throw on a nice outfit for when she finally does come back. I looked at my clothes that hadn't been stolen and made two different outfits. Neither of which I liked until I thought of mixing the two together. White T-shirt, black zip-up hoodie, midnight-blue super-skinny jeans, black Converse high tops, and a light-brown hooded jacket. I took a look to see how I looked in my now broken mirror until I remembered my mom telling me never to look into broken mirrors because it will give you bad luck. I guess I got a quick enough glance to see that I looked pretty fresh. Feeling surprised with myself, I decided to into my washroom where the mirror actually wasn't broken and decided to shave my face and put some Burberry aftershave, which was very surprisingly still there somehow! Looking in the mirror at myself, I thought, *Damn, I'm going to die a handsome motherfucker!* Then I figured it was time I figure out what kind of shoes and hat I'm going to wear. It didn't look too mucky or wet outside, so I decided to throw on my favorite pair of black leather Lacoste shoes that I had hidden. Thankfully, they didn't find them! Thank you for being so nice to me today, God! This couldn't be going any better. Actually, there is something that can in fact make this scene better: music! After putting on my shoes, I walked through the huge mess and walked into my room. The only hat they hadn't stolen was my LA Lakers one. It was a really nice hat, and I have no idea why they did not steal it. I decided then and there to wear my toque instead since we're going to be bussing and it'll be colder later on. Looking fresh as hell, I then went back into my kitchen to see if there was anything to snack on a little bit before going to dinner with Lola. I found frozen chocolate chip Eggos and milk with Raisin Bran cereal! Fuck yeah! This is going to be an absolutely perfect snack before this date that determines if I'm going to live or die. I was trying to put more thought into my suicide plan and try to maybe reason my way out of it. My mind just kept sliding away from the topic as a whole and kept going back to Lola. Man, I've got to be in love or crushing really badly because, wow, she's literally always on my mind. I feel passionate when I think about her and the way she smiles and laughs. Even though she and I have spent time together only just over a handful of times, it feels like I've known her for my whole entire life. She has such a powerful effect on me, and I absolutely love it. She's such a queen! Such a fucking babe of a queen, a beautiful emo queen, an angel who literally fell from the clouds and heavens above. Hopefully, I pray that it was destined that I meet her and eventually fall in love with her and then make her my partner. Tonight I shall know for sure. We just have to get some drinks going and hopefully some pot. Throw some Valium in the mix, and you'll have a good night! Believe me, I out of all people would know. I started making my "snack" and looked through my liquor hiding spots, and I found some booze! Half a bottle of red wine and about just under half a bottle of vodka. Awesome sauce! I made my breakfast of a snack and ate it up really quick because I didn't want Lola to come back and catch me eating to which would probably lead her to thinking I'm not down for dinner anymore. And what do you know? As soon as I put all the dirty dishes in the sink, I heard a knock on the door. You guessed it, 'twas pretty little Lola! Fuck to the yeah!

"Sup, gorgeous?" I asked when I saw her standing there.

"Oh wow, look at you! I really like your outfit, especially your shoes," she said.

"Thank you! I figured since I'm going on a date with you, I might as well look as sharp as you always do," I said with a grin as I let her inside my dump yard bachelor pad.

"Oh, aren't you just the sweetest person on the whole planet," she said somewhat sarcastically, which bothered me a little bit.

"So how was your hangout with your friend?" I asked her.

"It was really good, and also, that reminds me. I brought a little bit of something back for us," she said as she went into her purse.

"What kind of surprise?" I asked in wonder.

"This," said Lola as she pulled out a full micky of rum and two liters of cola.

"Oh, damn! Good thinking, then we won't have to buy as many drinks when we're there," I said, realizing how good of an idea it was.

"Do you have any shot glasses?" she asked me.

"I actually do, believe it or not. I'll be right back!" I said as I stepped over lots of trashed stuff to go into the kitchen. "Here you go!" I said when I came back and gave her both shot glasses.

"Thank you, dear," Lola said with a perfect smile on her face.

She filled both shot glasses with rum, and I also brought back a couple glass for pop to use as chase.

"Here's to us going to dinner tonight!" said Lola.

"Here's to us, period," I said.

I wish I hadn't said that because it definitely made things really weird and awkward. Lola didn't even say anything back either, which made it even more awkward! Fuck me! We clinked glasses and took our shots. Then Lola immediately poured out two more shots for us, and we took them almost literally right after the first two. I couldn't believe this at first, but she ended up pouring a third round of shots for us at which I somewhat intervened.

"Okay, hold up. We're not taking round three like now, are we?" I asked, hoping she would say no.

"No…if you're a massive pussy!" she said, laughing.

"It's just, we're going out to dinner, so I don't think we should be like completely black out drunk, you know what I mean? I don't want either of us to end up getting sick too. Especially at the restaurant. I mean, wouldn't that be humiliating or what?" I tried explaining to her.

"Ah, all right then, I guess," she said, seeming a little disappointed.

"Oh, come on, pumpkin. We'll take those shots very shortly, but first, I think we should decide on where we're go to eat," I said, hoping it would cheer her up a bit.

"Umm, I'm not too sure. Do you have any cravings for anything in particular?" she asked me.

"Do you like sushi?" I asked back.

"No, I fucking hate fish. Sorry, ha ha ha," she answered.

"East Indian?" I asked, feeling hopeful about some butter chicken.

"Is that the one with curry, and it's super spicy and shit?" she asked.

"Yes, it is indeed that shit," I answered.

"I'm not the biggest fan, to be honest," she answered.

"Okay, how about I ask you what kind of food you like?" I asked. "Because I'm down for whatever, but maybe there are some categories of food you must like." I was feeling kind of annoyed, almost.

"Umm, I don't know. I like Italian," she said to me.

Wow, really? Italian? I thought. *Fuck sakes. I just went to Olive Garden with Lizzy, and now Lola's craving Italian. Nice.*

"Yeah, okay. Why not?" I said, trying to hide the fact that I wasn't really digging the idea.

"Why don't we do Olive Garden or something. I haven't been there in forever!" said Lola as she was now very excited about dinner.

I cannot fucking believe this…not only does she want Italian, but she *also* wants to go to the one and only Olive Garden! What are the odds of this really happening? Fuck sakes.

"Now I'm really excited! I'm going to get fettuccine or something like that!" she said, practically salivating about the idea.

"I'm not 100 percent sure what I'm going to have. It's been a while, and I need to check their menus," I said, obviously knowing that I was there with Lizzy only a few nights ago.

"All right. Well, I'm just going to put on a different shirt with shoes, and I'll be ready to go!" said Lola as she made her way to the door.

"Don't forget to grab a jacket and maybe a scarf or toque," I reminded her.

"Ouu, didn't think of that! Thanks, Vince," she said as she stepped out of my place and went to her side of the duplex.

Damn, she didn't call me Vinny like I hoped she was going to. Pretty rough start to a date that I was really looking forward to. Keep it together, Vin!

"You ready to go?" asked Lola as she stood by the door.

"I'm ready. But do you still want to take these last shots?" I answered back with a question.

"Oh, right! Shit, I completely forgot about those, ha ha!" she said as she laughed and walked into the living room.

"Yeah, let's take these and then go!" I said to her.

We both took our shots, and then Lola asked me if I wanted to smoke a joint with her before we leave for dinner. I was very relieved that she offered and had some weed because whoever broke in took my bong, pipe, weed, grinder, papers, everything! Like I said earlier, if I ever found these mother fuckers, I think I would honestly kill them. I had three altars for each of my family members, but now they're all smashed up. Anyways, Lola pulled out a very nice joint out of her jacket pocket, and we both smoked it down to a tiny roach size before deciding to get rid of it and go to Olive Garden. We both ended up taking a fourth shot each and then finally exited the house. We both made sure that both of our places were locked before finally walking down toward the bus stop.

"It's actually not too bad out today," I said just to break the ice.

"Yeah, this fall has been really warm compared to recent years," replied Lola.

"I couldn't agree more. Usually, it's freezing, wet, and super windy but this year is really different," I stated.

As we were talking about the weather, we both looked up and saw that the bus that we needed to catch literally just drove by us… Fuck, I absolutely hate it when that happens! You always get so close and then *boom*, it comes out of nowhere and just blows by right in front of you. We were both pretty bummed but agreed that neither of us minded waiting another ten to fifteen minutes for the next one.

"Shit, I can't believe that just happened!" said Lola as we made it to the bus stop.

"No kidding, right? It always happens to me too, which I think is bullshit," I replied.

"Damn, I'm sorry to hear that. Don't you have a bus app or anything like that on your phone?" she asked. "Don't worry, there'll be another one soon because it's a weekday anyways."

"Yeah, I know you're right. Do you need a cigarette?" I asked her.

"I would love one since I just remembered that I forgot my own pack at home. Fuck!" said Lo as she couldn't find her pack anywhere.

"No worries, my dear," I said as I opened my pack and saw that there were only two smokes left. Shit.

"Thank you so much!" she said.

"Okay, so, I'm completely out of smokes now, and I need to hit up 7-Eleven for more. I doubt the next bus will be here in five minutes, don't you?" I told Lola.

"Okay, I'll wait here, just in case the bus comes and tell the driver to wait until you come back," Lola said, making me feel disappointed and somewhat depressed.

"Perfect," I exclaimed.

I then turned my back on her. As I walked toward 7-Eleven, I realized that this date had a pretty rough start, to say the least. This almost feels like the bipolar opposite of when Lizzy and I went on our little dinner date. Everything seemed perfect that day with Liz, so why can't today be nice for me and Lola. Very heartbreaking shit, if you ask me. I made my way inside the store and was greeted by the two East Indian people working there. The whole place was empty and almost dead silent. As soon as I got my pack of smokes and went outside, I looked up and saw the bus coming to the stop where Lola was.

"Thanks for waiting!" I said to the bus driver before getting on.

Lola found some empty spots at the back of the bus, and we both sat there together. There were a lot of people on the bus, some of them were homeless as fuck and smelled like piss. It's especially times like these when I really wish I didn't have a DUI and had my car and license instead. The homeless guy sitting in front of us smelled so bad that both Lola and I had to cover our mouths and noses. He was also passed out drunk and his pants soaked in his own piss. Lola then went digging inside her purse and pulled out two black Sharpie markers.

"Are you for real right now?" I asked very quietly, trying not to laugh.

"Fuck, yeah. Let's do it!" said Lola.

She gave me one of the Sharpies, and we both started drawing penises on the homeless guy's neck. I drew a swastika on his forehead, and Lola drew pentagrams on his cheeks. I swear to God, Lola and I are meant to be together. It's moments like that which make you realize you've met your cosmic twin, your cosmic lover. We finally arrived at the bus stop we had to get off on and left that homeless guy with a complete makeover! Poor old bastard.

"Fuck, yeah, we're almost there!" said Lola, who she seemed very excited about dinner.

"Hells to the yeah, baby. Nothing like some good old Italian food," I said even though I wasn't craving Italian in the slightest.

"I'm glad you're finally out of the ward and feeling better," she said.

"Thanks, I know this may sound odd, but being in there because you're crazy usually tends to make you even more crazy…" I explained to Lola.

"Honestly, I don't think that's odd at all. If anything, that's a really good quote, and I think you should write it down!" said Lola, seemingly impressed by the on-the-spot quote I came up with.

"Gee, thanks, Lo!" I said as I all of a sudden started to think of my plans for later on in the evening.

"There it is! Yay!" said Lola as she started skipping over to the restaurant.

Lola looked like an angel. The way she spoke, the way she moved, hell, even the way she smelled, was perfect! She was my dream girl but 2.0.

We made our way inside the restaurant, and luckily, there wasn't too much of a line inside. We were given a beeper and were told that the waiting time was about ten to fifteen minutes. We both decided to go outside to have a final smoke before my "last supper." It seemed like the perfect night to sit in your bedroom, stick the barrel of a shotgun into your mouth, and pull the trigger. It also seemed like the perfect night to be alive as well. Decisions, decisions…

"So are you and your boyfriend still together or…" I decided to ask since I realized I had absolutely nothing to lose anyways.

"Fuck no! He's completely lost his mind, and at this rate, I don't think he will ever get it back," she replied.

"I guess that makes you single then, right?" I asked.

"Single and ready to mingle," she replied with a suggestive smile on her face.

See, this is the problem with borderline personality disorder. You think that people either love you to death or hate your guts. No middle ground whatsoever. You tend to fall in love extremely easily because it's black and white in your head, so you think either this person loves you or hates you. Judging by the fact that Lola doesn't hate me and is talking about being single and ready to eat Pringles, whatever the fuck that means, I immediately start thinking that oh yeah, we're not only going to fuck, we're going to date! Nah, even better, married! And then beyond! Into the afterlife without a single thing throughout the entire ordeal going wrong. Sounds a little too good to be true, right? Believe me, I know.

Both Lo and I finished our cigarettes, and our beeper went off. We went back inside the restaurant and were seated by a hostess. We sat there for a little while in an awkward silence before Lola began a conversation.

"So how long have you and Lizzy been together?" she asked me.

"Oh, we're not together. Used to be years ago but not anymore," I replied.

"Why not?" asked Lola.

"I don't know. Time, I guess," I said.

"What do you mean by time?" she asked me.

"Well, you know what it's like being in a relationship. In the start, it's all good and nothing ever goes wrong. But then, as time passes and the more you and your partner get used to each other, you also become bored and that's when arguments begin, and then threats, and then boom! End of the relationship," I explained, setting a very dark tone for the dinner we were about to enjoy.

"Yeah, I agree. When Chad and I began dating, it was so dreamlike, everything was great. Until one night. I was at a party with him, and I got way too fucked up. Molly, alcohol, Xanax— the whole nine yards almost. I made out with one of my female friends, and honestly, I didn't think it would affect too much considering it was with another female. But no, he took me outside, into his car, and silently drove us home as I cried and kept saying sorry and sorry again."

"Go on," I suggested.

"We got home and after getting inside—oh, this is before you moved in below us too by the way—anyways, he took me into the living room and told me how he felt about it and asked me if I wanted to 'feel the pain.' I said 'yes' because I knew I deserved it. However, instead of calling or texting up some girl to make out with or fuck to get even with me, he punched me in the face *so* fucking hard. I literally hit the ground immediately. I couldn't really see out of my left eye for a while, and then he sat on top of me and cracked me in the face two more times and said, 'That's what the pain felt like,'" explained Lola, almost starting to tear up.

"Jesus, that is so fucked up...I'm so sorry that happened, Lo," I said.

"He said that if I ever told someone, he would kill me," Lola said, before grabbing a napkin to gently wipe her eyes with gently.

"Well, that's not going to happen, and you know that, Lo. They got him locked in pretty well at the ward. There's no way he could escape from there," I said to her, in hopes that it would cheer her up.

"Sometimes I still feel like there's something or someone that's out to get me," she admitted.

"Do you feel like someone's watching you or spying on you?" I asked her.

"Kind of, yeah. I feel this dark presence as if it's coming closer to me, and then it feels like it's so close that it's right behind or beside me," she said.

"I grabbed my bottle of Valium on the way out, do you need some by chance?" I asked with a large grin stretching across my face.

My Stupid, Sad, Pathetic Life

"Are you fucking kidding me? You had Valium this whole time, and you didn't tell me? Vincent, Vincent, Vincent, what are we going to do with you?" she asked in sarcasm.

"See, at first I was going to give you three, but you just talked your way down to one, sissy missy," I said to her, trying not to laugh.

"Sissy missy? Really? Open your mouth, I need to go pissy. How about that?" said Lola with a grin on her face now as well.

"That, honestly, sounds really fucking hot!" I admitted, with boner forming in seconds! I had to cross my legs when the waiter finally came to our table.

"Hey, guys! How are you doing tonight?" asked the waiter. "Really nice night for a date, hey?"

"Oh, we're not dating. We're just friends," said Lola, absolutely shattering my heart.

"Sorry, she has a really great sense of humor sometimes," I said to the waitress in self-defense.

"Ha ha ha ha! That's awesome. What can I get for you guys to drink tonight?" asked the waitress.

"I'll have a rum and Coke, please!" requested Lola.

"Sounds good, and for yourself?" the waitress asked me.

"I think I'll have a scotch on the rocks, please and thank you," I replied to her.

"Sounds good! I'll bring you guys your breadsticks and drinks in a moment."

"Thank you!" said Lola.

"Thanks," I said to her as she walked away from our table.

Both Lola and I went quiet for a little while. She was looking at her phone, and I was looking around the restaurant, checking out different couples at different tables with different dishes and drinks. Despite being here not too long ago, I must admit, this place does have a nice vibe to it.

"So what are your plans for the rest of the night?" I decided to finally ask.

"Probably nothing. I was thinking about playing with my Ouija again though, ha ha," she answered.

"You feel like a dark presence is coming near you or close to you, and you still play that game? I mean, I'm no specialist or anything, but from what I've heard, it's like opening a portal to another realm," I said.

"I know! That's the best part about it, you can talk to the ghost of Kurt Cobain if you tried hard enough," she said.

"I bet you can, no crap," I said.

"Other than that, I don't really know. Probably smoke some weed and watch something. Maybe hit the hay earlier, not 100 percent," she said back to me.

"Sounds like a good time," I said.

"Yeah, I might have a friend over. Known him since junior high," she said.

Wow, I guess I am blowing my brains out tonight after all…

Chapter 14

Fuck, as if! This is fucking bull to the shit. I'm literally on a "date" with Lola, but yet she "might" be having a male friend over? Like give me a fucking break. Seriously? I'm so mad right now, and this is stupid. I mean, why are we even on a date if she's just going to sleep with some other guy afterward? I'm not fucking paying her bill, and I hope she knows that. The waitress then came back with our fuck-boy bread sticks and stupid-ass drinks. Fuck, I'm so mad right now.

"Okay, guys, here are your drinks and breadsticks! Have either of you made any decisions on what you'd like for dinner? If not, it's no problem. I can give you more time," said the waitress to us.

The last thing I need is more time in awkward silence with this absolutely gorgeous queen of a woman who apparently isn't into me after all. So goddamn fucking stupid, other than seeing my family again and fulfilling my dream destiny.

"Yeah, I'm actually ready to order!" I said, knowing I hadn't even looked at the menu.

"Okay, great! What'll it be tonight?" she asked.

Not Lola, I thought. I pretended that I forgot which dish I wanted to enjoy, so I had an excuse to crack open the menu. Lola gave me a really weird look. *What are you looking at?* I thought as I made eye contact with her for a brief second.

"I'll have this four cheese pasta entrée right here," I said to the waitress as I pointed it out on the menu.

"Oh, that's one of my favorites!" said the waitress.

"Isn't it absolutely wonderful?" I asked her with a smile on my face. At this point, I wanted Lola to feel like something is wrong.

"I recommend you put some parmesan cheese on top! It's like the cherry on top of the icing on the cake, you know?" she said to me, giggling.

"Cheese, that's a lot of cheese!" I said with a flirty look on my face.

She laughed so hard, and immediately, I could tell that this was making Lola feel a little bit uncomfortable. Perfect. My plan is working.

"And have you made a decision yet, my dear?" the waitress asked Lola.

"Yes. Actually, I have," she said, and this threw me off guard. "I'm just going to have a Caesar salad tonight. Trying to lose some weight, you know how it is."

Ouch! Lola literally just called the waitress fat and completely changed the feel of the energy in the room, maybe even the whole restaurant. Damn, maybe I took it a little too far.

"Sounds good, darling," said the waitress to Lola.

She left our table, and boy, I thought it was awkward before, but now? Holy shit, it literally felt as if the whole restaurant got quiet and less "vibrant," if that makes any sense. I figured pulling out my phone and pretending to text someone would at least make it seem like I'm doing something. And hey, what do you know? Lizzy texted me! She said that she hopes I'm doing okay and glad you're out of the hospital. Oh, Lizzy. How I miss those times when we were together.

"I need to hit the little ladies' room. I'll be right back," stated Lola.

She got up and walked away from the table as if she was never going to look back ever again. This is actually fucking brutal. This whole night has honestly been so shitty now that I think about it. This date was never destined to be, and neither were Lola and I. I literally thought I was going to start crying at the dinner table. Keep it together. After this, you're going to see your family again! Who cares about Lola and this shitty reality I live in? Not me, that's who. I replied to Lizzy before putting my phone in my pocket and waited for Lola to get back from the bathroom. Fuck, I can't wait for this dinner to end. Of course, the waitress came by with Lola's salad right away because salad is pretty quick to make compared to pasta. She asked if everything was okay, and I said yes, even knowing that deep down, nothing was okay. I sat there waiting and waiting, and finally, I could see Lola making her way back to the table.

"Oh, gnarly! My salad is here!" she said with a forced fake smile on her face.

"Is everything okay?" I asked, knowing I was going into dangerous territory.

"Yeah. Everything's fine. Are you okay, Vincent?" she asked, giving me a death stare.

"Perfectly fine over here. You just seem a little tense," I managed to say, regretting it immediately.

"Yeah. You know what? Maybe you're right," she said before grabbing her almost full rum and Coke and pounding it back in only three gulps!

"Damn, girl," I said, now feeling beyond awkward and kind of lost as of what to do or say next.

"You still haven't given me those Valiums either," she said as if she was entitled to them or something.

"Here you go," I said after pulling my bottle out of my pocket and grabbing two for her.

"I thought you said three?" she asked.

Seriously? Wow. She is in complete bitch mode at the moment. This is not turning out good at all!

"Here," I said as I openly placed the whole bottle in the middle of the table so everyone in the restaurant could see.

She snatched the bottle in a second and gave me a really dirty look. This fake date can end at any moment now. I hope it's sooner than later because this is the bipolar opposite of what I was hoping was going to happen tonight.

"Thanks," she said after popping two or three of them and handing me my bottle back.

"No problem," I said, trying to at least sound like I was oblivious to the downfall of this date.

"Now I just need a refill, and I'll be okay," she stated.

I decided to say nothing. I also figured, if she's getting a refill, I may as well too. While watching Lola quickly eat up her salad, I grabbed my scotch and chugged the whole glass down. I don't know why, but it felt like everyone in the restaurant was looking at us. I felt as if the negative energy that Lola and I conjured up spread throughout the room and everyone could tell where it was coming from. Like a really wet, pre-poop fart, you know? The ones that not only smell like a rotting fetus but linger around and spread throughout the whole place.

"How's your salad?" I decided to ask Lola.

"It's really delicious, thanks for asking," she replied coldly.

"I'm glad to hear that," I said, hoping the awkwardness would stop, but I was wrong.

She didn't end up saying anything, and I immediately assumed that there's no way to turn this one around. Now I really couldn't wait for my pasta to arrive. Too bad I'm going to have to eat my "last supper" very quickly because I'm sure Lola doesn't want to stick around here or with me any longer. Then in the distance I saw our waitress, and she was coming toward us.

"Hey guys! How's the salad?" the waitress asked Lola.

"Oh, it's absolutely incredible, really hitting the spot, thank you. Oh, can I also get a refill please?" she asked.

"Of course, and for yourself, sir?" she asked me.

"Yes, please. If you don't mind," I answered.

"Sounds good to me! Also, your food will be ready soon," she said to me.

"Awesome, thank you so much!" I said to her, hoping she didn't feel the negative energy emitting from this table.

"No worries!" she said as she walked away.

"So what are your plans tonight?" Lola asked me, putting emphasis on "your."

"I think I might write something to be perfectly honest," I replied.

"You're going to write something? Like what?" she asked.

"I'm not too sure yet. It might just be an entry in my journal, or it may be a poem. Perhaps an outline with ideas for a book to write. Or maybe, just maybe, a rap song!" I answered with sarcasm.

"Are you serious? A rap song? You can't be serious," she said, laughing lightly.

"Yeah, I wanted to be a rapper years back. Thought it would be cool to be rich and famous," I told her.

"Why a rapper though?" she asked.

"Well, let's just say for the last few years, everyone has wanted to become a rapper. I wanted to make it big because I love music, and I loved making it. With rap being so violent and scary and overall terrible for the last while now, I thought it would be interesting to try and change the rap game through peace and love," I explained as I saw the waitress coming with our drinks and my entrée.

"All right, guys, here are your refills and here is your pasta! Is there anything else I can grab for the two of you?" asked the waitress.

"Nope!" I said.

"Nadda," replied Lola.

"All right then, enjoy!" she said to us as she finally walked away.

"Sweet! This looks awesome!" I said as I looked at my dish.

"That is some really interesting stuff indeed. You never struck me as a rapper or even a writer to be honest," she stated.

"Well, now you know," I said, forcing a fake smile.

Lola got started on her drink and the rest of her salad as I ate my pasta. It was delicious, but at the same time I couldn't even taste it. All of a sudden, the room got really quiet and the lights dimmed. I couldn't hear Lola or understand what she was saying to me. I was splitting. And not only that, it had a light touch of psychosis to it. I started feeling bad for Lola. I thought of her fucking her guy friend and then all of a sudden hearing a loud shotgun blast from below and then discovering me with no face or head. I felt so bizarre that I had to interrupt Lola even though I didn't know what she was talking about and go to the washroom. I walked into the washroom, and the floors and walls were breathing. Fuck! As if this date couldn't get any worse…like what are the fucking odds of this night turning out this brutally? Fucking horseshit. Of course, I only brought my Valium and not my clozapine. I decided to splash my face with water and then look into the mirror. Looking up to face the mirror, I didn't see my reflection. Instead, I saw my mom, dad and sister standing in a beautiful field of green with a perfect blue sky above.

"Do not waste anymore time, son. Jesus has seen your struggles throughout life, and he knows that you are in danger," my father said to me.

"Come, please join us, Vincent. Please, honey," my mom said, making tears fall down my face.

"What do you mean, danger?" I asked them.

"Just come and be with us already, Vinny. I miss you so much," said my sister.

"You can be with us if you choose, Vincent, and you can choose as soon as you want. You can choose between that or having your soul sucked into hell. Which do you choose?" explained my father before asking.

"I want to be with you guys. I don't want to be here anymore," I said.

"Well then, you know what you need to do son. Now go and do it," said my father with a smile on his face.

"Okay. I will. I love you guys so much, and I'll see you soon," I said to them, completely crying my eyes out and feeling incredibly happy.

All of a sudden, they disappeared and I could see my own reflection in the mirror. There was a guy who was standing beside me who looked somewhat concerned and confused. Or at least I assume so.

"Yo, dude, are you like okay?" he asked me, sounding and looking really tripped out.

"I have never been better, my dude," I calmly replied to him while wiping my eyes dry. "Thanks for asking though!"

"Yeah, um, no problem," he said as I walked out of the washroom.

I felt incredible. I felt so happy. And I felt like leaving the restaurant immediately, going home, and blowing my fucking brains out. Or, even better, I'm going to hit the nearby skate park one more time because I remember my dad always telling me to get into skateboarding and to get good at it because it would make a lot of girls like me. For the most part, he was definitely right. Good old pops. I got to the table, sat down, and whipped out my wallet. I saw the waitress across the room and flagged her down.

"How can I help you?" she asked me.

"I'm actually going to get this boxed up for the go because I have this thing which I forgot about and it's really important. You know, life stuff," I said.

"Okay, no worries, I'll get this boxed up for you," she said, sounding a little confused and surprised.

"Are you, okay, Vincent?" Lola asked very slowly while giving me a weird look.

"Yeah, I'm fine! I received a call from a friend I used to skate with when I was in the bathroom, and I really want to link up with them," I replied.

"You're going to go skateboarding at night in this weather? Seriously?" she asked me. "What's really going on, Vince?"

"I'm going skating with this friend because I miss them and I want to see them," I managed to say.

"Who is this person you need to see oh so badly?" she persisted.

"Her name is Joyce, and she's really good at skateboarding. She's also really nice to talk to about life and how hard and shitty it is," I said to her, literally pulling that lie right out of my ass.

"Joyce, hey? Old girlfriend or just skater friend?" she asked.

"Well, we did hook up a few times at a couple of parties and stuff, but that's pretty much it," I said, lying like crazy again.

"Hmm, interesting," said Lola, sounding somewhat disappointed.

"Also, I don't want to keep you waiting here while I eat my food. You need to see your friend or whatever anyways, right?" I said to her, trying to cheer her up. Fuck, I can be really cold sometimes.

"Right! Yeah, life stuff, ha-ha," she said.

The waitress finally came with my boxed-up pasta and a debit machine.

"Are we splitting this two ways, guys?" she asked us.

"No, actually. I'm paying for everything," I stated.

"Wait, what! You don't have to pay for my food," said Lola.

"Oh no, I absolutely insist," I insisted.

"That's so sweet!" said the waitress. Not that money matters to me anymore.

I paid the bill of nearly $100 while Lola was staring at me, trying to figure out what was really up with me.

"And would you like a copy of your receipt?" she asked.

"Yes," said Lola right at the exact same time as I said no.

"Seriously, I'm going to pay you back I swear, Vince," she said.

"Here you go! I hope you guys have a wonderful evening, thanks for coming!" the waitress said to us as she handed me my copy and walked away.

Both Lola and I stood up at the exact same time. It was definitely kind of awkward. We both put our jackets on in complete silence and made our way out of the restaurant. We barely said anything to each other on the bus ride home, but I didn't care too much considering I'm going to join my family again after "skating with Joyce," ha ha ha! Oh! A terrific idea just hit me! I'm going to get some smack while I'm at it since I won't be alive for long! I texted my dealer and got myself a chop lined up. Now I really can't wait to finally get home! We got off at our stop and walked in complete silence all the way back to our place.

"All right, well, I should get my deck and get going," I suggested.

"Oh, yeah I don't want to keep you waiting or anything," she said, seemingly kind of sad all of a sudden.

"Bye, Lola," I said, trying not to raise suspicion.

"Bye, Vince," she said and once again, sounding sad now.

We both got into our own places without even a hug or chance of a kiss. I tried to not care about it, but I couldn't. C'mon, all I need to do is just think of her fucking her guy friend. Yeah, that'll probably work! I quickly went into my bedroom and grabbed my skateboard and then headed out just as fast. I hopped on my board and skated all the way to the park. I saw that there were three teenagers who were all skating, drinking beer, and smoking weed. Gnarly! I hopped back on my board and tried doing some basic tricks like the ollie, shove-it, kickflip, and heelflip. My first attempt was a kickflip, and I did it, but the landing wasn't very clean. I tried a heelflip next and same thing, nailed it but with a dusty landing. I kept looking over at the three teens because all of a sudden, I had a really bad feeling in my stomach and not only that, they were looking at me. I thought about dipping right then and there but decided not to because this is it! This is the last time I will ever skateboard. I can stay as long as I want. I kept going around and over and over the outskirts of the park and using new tricks each time I went around.

"Nice board, dude," said one of the teens who were now uncomfortably close to me.

"Oh hey, thanks," I said awkwardly and slowly.

"Our buddy here doesn't have a skateboard," said the same teen.

"Damn that sucks. There's lots of places that sell them, you know," I said to them.

"No. We're not going to buy one, we're going to steal one," said the teen.

"Well, good luck then. Security is pretty tight on skateboards these days," I stated.

"No. We're going to steal your skateboard!" said the teen as his friends laughed.

"Oh, fuck off, no way. I'm going to kill myself tonight, and I wanted to have a last skate before doing so," I explained, feeling worried.

"Aw, isn't that adorable?" said one of them.

Two of them distracted me as one went behind me and cracked me over the head with his skateboard trucks. My legs collapsed beneath me, and just like that, I was on the ground, bleeding from the head while being stomped out by three teenagers. Wow, I am *definitely* doing it tonight! The beating lasted like five minutes, but damn, they messed me up good. My clothes were dirty and wet, plus I had cuts and bruises all over my face and body. My nose was like a waterfall of blood. It wouldn't stop, and it was all over my clothes. I got up after lying there for a good four to five minutes and realized that they had taken my phone and wallet along with my skateboard. Now I, without any doubt, have any purpose to live. I walked home and even cried a little bit on the way there. I was happy that I was only moments away from being with my family again.

Chapter 15

I walked onto the property and saw Lola sitting on the front steps while smoking a cigarette and talking to someone on the phone. As I walked closer to the front steps, I could see that Lola developed a dropped jaw due to the fact that I looked like I got hit by a bus. I just kept looking down at the ground and walked past Lo until she hung up on the phone and stood up.

"Dude, what the fuck!" she said, sounding afraid.

"It's nothing to worry about, you know? Don't worry," I said as I tried to get my house key until I realized those fools stole it. Fuck!

"Vincent, what the actual fuck happened to you?" Lola asked in a sassy tone.

"Don't worry, I just got everything else remaining in my life stolen from me, that's all," I said as I walked over to the living room window because it was smashed and I could get in that way.

"Vincent, seriously! What the fuck happened to you?" she asked in a demanding manner.

"Look, it doesn't fucking matter, okay?!" I yelled as I turned around. "Nothing fucking matters anymore, okay?! Look at my life! I'm going to my bedroom, and I'm going to try to go to sleep."

"You're just going to go to bed?" she asked.

"Yeah. I don't want to be in this reality at the moment, so I'm going to pop some Valium and melatonin and go to another place, a better place," I lied straight to her face.

"You mean, a dream, right?" she asked, looking confused as hell.

"Something like that, yeah," I responded.

"You're not going to do anything stupid, are you?" she asked me.

"The last thing I'm going to do is something stupid, okay?" I said, realizing how weird of a statement that was.

"You promise?" she asked with authority.

"Yup," I said calmly.

"Pinky swear?" she insisted.

"Yup," I repeated.

"Seriously, Vince!" she yelled.

"I won't! Okay?!" I yelled back.

We both looked away from each other with angry faces and went into our separate places. Once I climbed through my almost completely smashed living room window, I went straight into my room and grabbed the shotgun from between the mattress as well as the bullets. I started loading up my father's shotgun, and I was honestly very happy that I was going to blow my whole face off and see my family again. The shotgun was all loaded and ready for action. I decided to look down the barrel of the gun, and I could see a light at the end instead of darkness. I could see that my family was there! And not only that, but they were waving at me! All right, this is it! Good-bye, planet Earth. I stuck the shotgun in my mouth and decided to count to ten before pulling the trigger and leaving this terrible place. Five…four…three…two…one…

Boom!

What the fuck?! I haven't even pulled the trigger. What the fuck was that noise?

Boom!

I heard it again, and it sounded like someone broke into Lola's place and started bolting up her stairs.

"Who the fuck? Don't touch me! *Ahhhhh! Help me!*" Lola screamed from upstairs.

"You got to be fucking kidding me… The minute I decide to end my life, Lola just happens to get kidnapped for fuck sakes?!" I said to myself, feeling very irritated and full of rage.

I could hear Lola screaming as the intruders carried her down her stairs.

"*Help me, Vincent! Help!*" she screamed before they stuck something in her mouth so she couldn't scream anymore.

I left my dad's shotgun on my bed and ran into my living room to see who the fuck was abducting Lola. I poked my head out my living room window to try and get a look at who exactly it was, and I couldn't believe what I saw. It was those fucking Satanists from the cemetery! Those creepy motherfuckers who chased us! All right, okay, you want to interrupt my fucking suicide? Okay then, I'm going to go out like Tony Montana, I decided. I stormed out of my living room and back into my bedroom. I grabbed my father's shotgun, his 9mm pistol, and his hand blade that I used to cut myself with. I found the strap that attaches to the shotgun and put it on. I put the knife in one of my back pockets, I put the handgun in between my belt just above my tiny penis, and I put the shotgun on so it was hanging off my back. I found my big trench coat and threw it on to cover up the shotgun on my back. Locked and loaded, I opened my front door and left my place without even closing my door behind me. Then I realized something, I never got my last dose of heroin! And my dealer just happens to live on the way to the cemetery. Fuck, this couldn't have worked out any better! I went from speed walking to lightly jogging, and before I knew it, I was at my dealer's place. Fuck, I don't have my wallet though. I might have to hold my heroin dealer at gunpoint now. Fuck! Anyways, I knocked on his front door. The door opened seconds after.

"Yo, Vinny! I thought you weren't going to show up! I got a shot ready to go for ya," said Tyler, my dope dealer.

"Look, Tyler, as much as I'd love to sit here and shoot up with you and melt all night, I have business to take care of," I said to him.

"Well, are you at least going bang up with me?" he asked.

"Oh, fuck yeah. I need to get high before I go do my thing," I explained.

"Also, what the flying fuck happened to you? Did you get hit by a truck or something?" he asked, looking somewhat concerned. "You look like you could really use a shot, and what kind of business are you attending to?"

"Look, I just got stomped out by three teenagers at the skate park, and now someone just abducted the chick who lives upstairs in my duplex," I said as I rolled up my sleeve and placed the handgun on his coffee table.

"Oh my god! Dude what the fuck are you doing with that gun, dude?" Tyler asked, looking shocked all of a sudden.

I didn't answer him. Instead, I grabbed the needle on top of the table and a bloody rubber band that was lying on the floor. I hit my vein first try and pushed the needle full of smack right into it.

"Dude, first of all, that was my shot. And two, what the fuck is up with the gun?" he asked again.

My Stupid, Sad, Pathetic Life

"Listen, bro, I'm about to go turn up on some fools, and I needed to get high. I'm going to come back here in the next hour, and I'll pay you. Okay?" I explained.

"All right then. That was a $30 shot, just so you know," he said.

"Yeah, I could tell, ha-ha. I'm higher than a blimp right now," I said.

Tyler then walked me to the front door, and I put my dad's handgun back between my belt. He opened the door and let me out into the darkness. High as fuck, I literally started skipping to the church. I was skipping! Christ sakes. I finally arrived at the cemetery, and I could see two of those satanic cocksuckers standing in front of the crypt they came out of when they chased Lo and I a few days ago. That must be where they were keeping Lola. Time for some serious business. I managed to squeeze my skinny body through the gate and casually walked toward the crypt guarded by two Satanists.

"Good evening, gentlemen! What a beautiful night to just stand in front of a crypt inside a cemetery, ain't it?" I asked them with a huge smile on my face.

"Leave now!" one of them demanded.

"You're a funny guy, fool. A funny-looking guy too, to be perfectly honest," I said while I was laughing.

They both became silent and just turned to look at one another. The one on the left side of the crypt turned to face me. He was wearing a cow mask on his face and the other dickhead had a deer mask on. Cow head then started walking toward me. I pulled on the strap on my chest and just like that, I had the shotgun aimed right at him.

Boom! I shot him right in the stomach, and he literally went flying back ten yards…

Deer head tried to run up on me until I turned to him, and *boom*, I shot him right in the head, and it exploded like a watermelon dropped from ten stories high. I was covered in fuck boy blood, but I didn't care. I kicked in the door to the crypt and saw two more fools right behind the door. *Boom!* I blasted the one closest to the door, and the intestines from his insides sprayed all over the other asshole behind him. When his body dropped, *boom*, I blasted the second motherfucker in the arm and his whole arm went flying after detaching from his body. He screamed in pain until, *boom*, I fired at his chest; and his entire rib cage exploded in my face before his body hit the floor. Covered in blood, intestines, and even bits of bones, I went down the staircase, deeper into the crypt to find Lola. Carefully going down, a fuck face with a bear mask ran up to the bottom of the stairs.

"Who the fuck are you?!" he yelled.

"I'm beary sorry, sir," I said right before, *boom*, shooting him right in the head.

His head and mask exploded into tons of gory chunks that covered the floor, walls, and even the stairs. After finally making it downstairs, I walked down a long tunnel that led to a room. I realized that I had fired six shots and that I only had two left. Walking in, I quickly jumped back as I figured there may be some yoyos hiding around a corner. And I was right too! From the right side, a guy with a huge blade quickly appeared, and he started running toward me. I let him get a little closer to make him think he has a chance. *Boom*, that honestly almost split that guy into two pieces! Fuck, this is very stress relieving if anything besides crazy. Time for the final boss, Mr. Goat Head. I walked into the room and saw that it was a very large and circular in shape with a large pit of fire in the middle. Just above the fire was Lola tied up on a large cross that was ready to fall over into the fire, burning Lola to death. It also made her look like she was crucified. Jesus Christ! Literally though…

"Lola!" I yelled, but she wasn't conscious.

Then from behind the cross came the punk with the goat mask and he was holding a large and sharp-looking blade.

"You imbecile! Have you lost your ability to see?" he asked me.

"Listen, dick picker, you let that girl down from there or I'm going to blast you!" I replied.

"She's not who you think she is! She's fooled you! She's a witch. You've been fooled!" he said.

"Don't listen to him, Vincent. He's a crazy lying satanic freak, and he's going to kill me!" Lola yelled, now being awake.

"Any last words, chief?" I asked the Satanist.

"No! You cannot kill in this room! You will wake it up! Please, please I beg you. Please don't shoot me!" he begged, putting his blade down.

"Kill him, Vince! He's going to fuck you over!" Lola screamed at me.

I aimed my shotgun at him and, *boom*, right in the stomach. He flew back and hit the wall, all bloodied up. I ran toward Lola, and I was going to start untying the ropes around her wrists and body, but something started happening. All of a sudden the whole place started to shake, as if an earthquake was coming. I tried to keep my balance but failed and hit the floor. Then the shaking stopped, but I could not believe what I was seeing! The fiery pit in the middle of the room started spiralling, and it looked like there was a hole in the middle of it. Even worse, however, was what came out of that dark red, fiery pit: Diabolus, the demon from my fucking nightmare a few days ago! Holy fucking shit! I can't fucking believe it! I turned around to see Lola standing literally right behind me and not tied up anymore to the crucifix. I screamed and jumped incredibly high.

"Is that Vincent screaming like a little girl?" asked Diabolus.

"Lola, what the fuck!" I screamed out loud in pure shock.

"You should've just stayed home and killed yourself, Vinny. You could've been with your parents by now!" she said to me.

"How the fuck did you know about that?!" I said, feeling extremely afraid at this point.

"I know you inside out, Vinny. Just like I knew my ex-boyfriend, and the one before that and the one before that," she explained, forming a smile on her face.

"You stupid fool!" said the ugly-looking beast from hell.

"Lola, what the fuck…Look, I'm sorry for how I acted during dinner. I only reacted that way because I thought that maybe you liked me. I really like you, Lola. I'm in love with you. If our date went well, then I wouldn't have tried to kill myself. You were the only thing holding me back from killing myself. I think you're so amazing, and I want you in my life. I don't know what the fuck is happening right now, but I just want to get you and get out of here. Please, Lola!" I said, falling down to my knees and starting to cry.

"I'm really sorry about this, Vince. My friend over here needs a soul unless I want to leave with him. And let's just say he's not my type. So you know what that means!" she said, laughing with the demon.

"What the fuck! What are you? What in God's name are you?" I screamed.

"I'm a witch, Vincent. And I'm going to take your soul so I can sell it to DB over here in exchange for more power! Oh, Vincent, you were so close to seeing your whole family again. But you let your eyes deceive you. You poor little fucker," Lola said to me calmly while having a creepy smile on her face.

"No! Fuck no! Fuck you, I'm going to see them right now!" I yelled as I put my dad's shotgun in my mouth.

I pulled the trigger, but nothing happened... I forgot, I must have used all of the bullets! Fuck! This isn't happening right now! No! Fuck no! Thankfully, I realized I had my dad's pistol as well. And I haven't fired a single shot from it! I grabbed the pistol from my waist and put it into my mouth.

"Fuck you and you!" I yelled at Lola and the monster.

I pulled the trigger, and my fucking pistol got jammed! No! Fuck! This can't fucking be happening! No, I was so fucking close, fuck this! Lola and Diabolus both engaged in some very evil-sounding laughter, and I tried firing my pistol at the demon, but it wouldn't work! Fuck this, I grabbed my knife and tried stabbing myself in the stomach. On some fucking harakiri shit! I tried to stab myself, but something was stopping me. An invisible force wasn't letting me stab myself! I tried again and again, but it wouldn't work! Fuck! I can't believe this is happening! I was so fucking close to being with my family again once and for all, but I fell for this elaborate lie... God, please, please take my soul so I can reunite with my family and spend eternity with them! Please, God, please! I beg you!

"God is not here at the moment, Vincent," said Diabolus.

"God will not save you, Vince! Neither will Jesus, the Holy Spirit, or any angels! You had your chance, and you blew it! All you had to do was ignore me and kill yourself. Now you're going to spend eternity in a psych ward, and when you die, you will be in hell and not with your family!" Lola explained to me, looking more and more evil by the second.

Her skin became a bluish-green color and her eyes became dark red and very demonic like. Her nose grew big and so did her fingers and limbs in general. In just a few minutes, Lola went from being an absolutely beautiful-looking girl to an ugly, mean-looking demonic witch. I can't believe this is actually happening! Fuck sakes, no way! No fucking way! No, please God, let me out of this mess! Demonic Lola walked right up to me, and I tried pushing her back to no avail. She shoved me, and I fell on the floor. She saddled herself on top of me and went in to kiss me. I tried to turn away, but I wasn't able to. She kissed me right on my lips, and I could feel all of my life coming out of my mouth and into hers. It felt like all of my happiness, faith, desire for life, hope, and soul was literally being pulled out of my body. I felt more and more weak the longer she kept kissing me, until I literally had no life left in me. I was still alive but now without a soul. Lola finally got off me and walked away. I tried running toward her, but I was held down on the ground by an invisible force. Lola walked over until she was right in front of the demon and, believe it or not, proceeded to kiss him, transferring my soul from her body to the demon! It was a sight to behold and not only that, but I saw my family members in the room too. They were all standing together in a corner, and they were all crying.

"Vincent! What have you done?! You were so close to being with us! You promised you would be with us!" my mother said as she tried to hold back her tears.

"You fucking little fool! I told you that your spirit was mine!" stated the demon, and he and Lola engaged in evil laughter together.

"Fuck both of you!" I screamed as I grabbed my dagger off of the ground and started charging toward Lola.

"You're not going to hurt me, Vincent. I know you won't," Lola said calmly, smiling.

"Oh yeah? Check this out!" I screamed as I stabbed Lola right in the stomach.

The dagger went deep into her stomach, and she had the look of pure shock written all over her face. I tried twisting the dagger in her stomach, and her legs collapsed underneath her. She fell to her knees, bleeding out like crazy! Blood was also pouring out of her mouth, and I kind of felt bad about it. But I'm not going to let a witch steal my soul like that!

"How…how could you do this to me, Vincent?!" Lola cried out in agony.

"More like, how the fuck could you do this to *me*?!" I yelled back at her.

"If you hadn't killed that last Satanist, Diabolus could've taken his soul and not yours!" she tried explaining, coughing up blood and returning to her human form.

"Well, it's not too late!" I said. "Hey, Diabolus? How about we do an old switcharooni, you know? Soul for soul, how's that? I mean, which do you think would be better? The ugly, lame, boring, failed schizophrenic with nothing-to-live-for soul? Or the soul of a gorgeous and beautiful yet wicked witch whose powers are not only beyond astonishing but also shape-shifting! All while being a so-called seemingly normal-looking human being! I mean, sure, my soul is a soul but think about this for a second, big DB. Her soul is capable of abilities far beyond normal human abilities! She can also transform into different appearances and fool anyone right before their own eyes. And believe me, she definitely fooled my eyes. So here we go!"

"You son of a bitch!" screamed Lola.

"Oh, mighty Diabolus! Prince and protector of Lucifer's lake of fire and kingdom of hell! I here have an offer you simply can't refuse! An offer that would greatly benefit you and your mighty dark powers! In the name of the Holy Father, creator of all things, I ask that this prince of darkness and king of hell trade me back my soul in exchange for the soul, flesh, blood, and bones of the wicked witch presented before thee in this very moment! With the help of the Father, the Son, and the Holy Spirit all by my side, I command you Diabolus to return my soul to me for a much more powerful one!" I screamed at the demon while staring deep into its fiery red eyes.

"Don't do this, DB. You already have his soul!" Lola tried pleading.

"Her soul can get you more souls once you have her soul, Diabolus. This is a no brainer!" I yelled at the beast.

"Enough! I have made my decision, and I must say, I'm very surprised. Vincent, I thought I had you. But the way you proposed the offer, I must say, you do have very good business tactics! As impressed as I might be, I will put one condition on the deal before we shake on it," said the demon.

"Okay, what condition?" I asked bravely.

"I will trade you your soul back and take the witch's one instead. However, if you decide to kill yourself in an attempt to be with your family without living the full duration of your life, your soul will be mine! But if you do live out the amount of time left in your life, you will see your family again," he explained and offered to me.

I quickly glanced back over at my family while dealing with the demon and they were all shaking their heads yes. Fuck sakes…I wanted to be with them like immediately! My mother also always used to tell me that I was going to be the one who lives the longest in the family. Well, as shitty as it might be, I guess it'll be worth it in the end after all.

"Okay, fine. Let's shake on it, you big scary motherfucker!" I said to the demon as I laughed, surprised at my incredible confidence!

"Sounds good," said the massive beast.

I pulled out the dagger from Lola's stomach, and she fell over and lay on the ground as a buddle of blood slowly formed around her. The beast and I walked up to each other, and we shook hands. Two of his fingers were the size of my whole hand!

"All right. I'm sorry, sweetie, I'm going to take your soul now," said the demon as he turned around to face Lola and started walking toward her.

"*Nooo!* Diabolus, please! Please, please don't do this, please!" begged Lola as she was barely alive now from that stab wound.

"I'm sorry, munchkin. I'm giving his soul back to him and taking yours!" he said to her.

I looked at the corner that my family was standing in, and they were all so happy! They were all jumping up and down, seeming extremely excited to see how I managed to barely convince a big scary demon to give me my soul back, and just in time too! After the monster sucked Lola's soul out of her body, he walked toward me until he was standing right in front of me. He placed one of his massive fingers on my forehead, right where the third eye/sixth chakra is, and just like that, I could feel my soul coming back inside of me! I felt all the emotions nameable all at the exact same time, and the feeling was extremely euphoric! It felt like I had died and then been completely reborn again. I felt it! And my fuck, it felt so good! So…fucking…good! I felt so alive and happy, and I looked over to my family, and they were all crying tears of joy while in shock about the fact that I just bribed a powerful demon from hell! I felt so happy! The demon walked to the edge of the portal on the ground before jumping directly into it. It closed behind him in a couple seconds, and just like that, he was gone!

"You did the right thing, son. We'll be waiting for you, sweetheart. I'm so proud of you!" said my dad. He was smiling and crying with my mom and sister.

"We'll be waiting for you, love. Try to make the most of life until then, and don't, no matter what, kill yourself son," my mom said to me.

"We love you, Vinny!" my sister said to me while waving.

"I can't wait to see you guys again. I love you all and miss you, guys," I said to my family as they started fading away.

I started crying so hard! I am so excited and happy I'm going to see them again. I have never felt so powerful, grateful, and fulfilled in my whole life. I looked around at the gruesome scene that was left over. I could hear police sirens coming from a far distance away. I looked over at the still beautiful but now dead body of the witch Lola. I couldn't believe that she actually turned out to be a soul-sucking demon-fucking witch. I can't wait to hear what the cops are going to say about the story that I'll provide them with. The sirens were easy to hear now that the police were just outside of the catacombs. I decided to just go and sit in the corner and wait for the police to come downstairs and join me in the massive bloodbath I was a part of, well, completely responsible for, that is, ha-ha.

"What in the name of the Holy Father happened down here?" one officer asked in amazement and shock as they slowly came downstairs one by one.

Chapter 16

The police officers took their sweet ass time looking around the bloodied crypt. They didn't even notice me sitting in the corner for like a good four to five minutes. They told me to put my hands up and lie down facing the ground. I did what they commanded, and they ended up cuffing me and taking me out of the catacombs and into the back of a police car. I waited in the back of that police cruiser for at least forty minutes. It didn't feel that long because I was still high as fuck off of heroin and Valium. I felt literally no remorse for my actions. I tried saving Lola, but she ended up being a witch and almost taking my soul away from me. So, in other words, I could've just let the Satanists kill her and been with my family already. But no, I just had to go after her and now it feels like I'm not going to see my family members for a really long time. At least I'm going to see them, I guess. I just have to wait an incredibly long time and not commit suicide or else my soul will go to Diabolus the demon. Two of the officers ended up puking at the gruesome sight of the crypt, and I even ended up passing out and needing to go to a hospital. Two cops finally got into the cruiser I was sitting in the back of and started driving toward downtown to the main police headquarters. Once we got there, the two officers took me straight inside and put me inside of a holding cell. Once they left, I took off my jacket and sweater and folded them and placed them on the floor. I decided to sit on top of them and meditate until the officers returned. I ended up meditating for a good twenty-five to thirty minutes before the cops came back. They entered the room and were kind of thrown off by the fact that I was meditating and not having a full-blown panic attack.

"Get up and put your clothes back on," demanded one of the officers.

I did exactly that and then ended up sitting at the table in the corner of the room with them. They looked very confused and shocked by the fact that I was so relaxed.

"Okay, so your name is Vincent Caswell, correct?" asked an officer.

"That's my name, don't wear it out," I replied casually.

"Vincent, what the fuck happened tonight?" the other officer asked.

"Well, gentlemen, it's a very long story. But I am willing to tell you everything if you're willing to listen to the whole story," I replied to them.

"Our shifts just started, so please tell us everything that happened, and please don't lie. Just tell the truth, okay?" explained an officer.

"Okay, get your pen and pad ready, because this is a story and half!" I told them.

"Shoot," one of the officers said.

The two officers and I ended up staying in the holding cell for a good hour and a half as I explained my story and they took notes. They asked me a whole bunch of questions, and I answered every single one as truthfully as I could. After I had finished my story and they had no more questions for me, they basically told me that I'm probably going to be in a lot of trouble since I killed at least ten of those satanic bastards. I told them I tried saving Lola, but one of the Satanists ended up stabbing her to death before I could save her.

"So you were in your room and you heard screaming upstairs?" one of the officers asked.

"That's exactly what happened, yes," I answered.

"And how did you know that it was the Satanists who abducted the girl?" the other officer asked.

"Lola and I were at the cemetery less than a week ago, and we saw them performing some ritual. We were playing with Lola's Ouija board, and they saw us and chased us out of the cemetery. Other than that, I guess it was just my intuition that assumed she got abducted by those bastards," I explained to them.

"What were they trying to do to the girl?" they asked me.

"They were trying to kill her and ended up doing so because I was too late when I arrived to the scene," I said.

"Why do you think they wanted to kill her?" they asked me.

"Honestly, I'm not too sure. Probably something to do with their ritual," I answered.

"So you just showed up with a fully loaded shotgun and began killing them one by one?" an officer asked.

My Stupid, Sad, Pathetic Life

"Pretty much, yeah. I just wanted to save her life, but the Satanists told me she was a witch and that's why they were wanting to kill her so badly," I tried explaining.

"A witch?" asked one of the officers.

"That's correct, sir. A witch," I answered.

"That sounds pretty fucking hard to believe, you know," stated the other officer.

"Well, I'm sorry I didn't keep one of those fuckheads alive for you guys," I said to the officers.

"Do you suffer from mental illness, Vincent?" one of the cops asked me.

"Why, yes, yes, I do. I suffer from borderline personality disorder, schizoaffective disorder, and PTSD," I informed the officers.

"What were you doing exactly when you heard them abducting Lola?" they asked me.

"Honestly, I was about to commit suicide by blowing my head off with my dad's shotgun, you guys," I admitted truthfully.

"Why were you wanting to kill yourself, Vincent?" one of them asked.

"Because I want to be with my family. All of my closest family members are dead. Both my mom and dad committed suicide, and my sister died in a drunk-driving accident," I told them.

"You think killing yourself is the best thing to do, Vincent?" the other cop asked.

"Well, now it's not, that's for sure," I answered.

I ended up telling them my whole family story and how Lola was basically the only thing keeping me alive. I kept mentioning the fact that she was a witch, according to the Satanists, and that they were apparently doing the right thing by killing her. Both officers told me that the story I provided them with was absolutely crazy and that they were going to drop me off at the psych ward for further examinations. I ended up staying in that holding cell for at least a good two hours before they finally took me out, cuffed me, and threw me back in the back of their cruiser.

I really didn't want to have to go to jail or prison for killing about ten to twelve people, so I just kept saying that Lola was a witch and she was trying to steal my soul. Which, honestly, is the truth. I wish they had security cameras in that crypt. I would love to see the look on the faces of all these cops as a fucking demon literally came out of hell and tried taking me with him. Maybe it was for the better though. I know what I saw and heard, but nobody is going to believe me. Like seriously? A witch and a demon? There's not a chance that anyone would actually believe my story. Maybe some of the schizophrenics at the psych ward. But other than that, I don't think anyone will actually believe me.

I woke up inside one of the most secure and damage-proof rooms in the entire psych ward. I didn't even remember falling asleep or getting to the psych ward last night. My back was very sore from the rock-hard bed that I slept on. I ended up sitting up in bed, and only minutes after, a nurse and doctor came inside of my room. They asked me what happened last night, and just like I told two officers, I told the entire crazy-sounding story. Anyways, long story short, I'm locked in the psych ward for the rest of my life... I get two smoke breaks a day, but other than that, I am not allowed to leave my room at all. I know that it really sucks and that I'm going to have to wait in here for an extremely long time, but in the end, I'm going to be with my family again, and that's all I give a fuck about. I'm so grateful that I was able to convince the demon to take Lola's soul instead of mine and return mine to me. What a life... But I literally can't fucking wait to die! I decided to lie in my bed as it became evening time. A nurse came into my room and gave me all my medications that I have to take before bed. Way more meds than I used to be on, that's for sure.

"Is there anything else I can grab for you before you go to sleep, Vincent?" she asked me.

"No, I think I'll be okay for tonight," I answered.

"Okay, well I hope you have a great sleep, Vincent. And you know the drill, another nurse will come in and see you in the morning. Good night, Vincent!" she said to me.

"Thank you and good night to you as well," I replied.

She left the room shortly after, leaving only me, myself, and I in it. Or so I thought. Just before I decided to tuck myself in after turning out the light, my dad appeared in the darkest corner of the room.

"Hey, Daddy," I said calmly.

"Hello, Vincent. I just wanted to wish you a good night and tell you that I love you," he said to me, smiling.

"I love you too, Dad. I love you so fucking much," I said, before lying all the way back in my bed and falling asleep.

The End

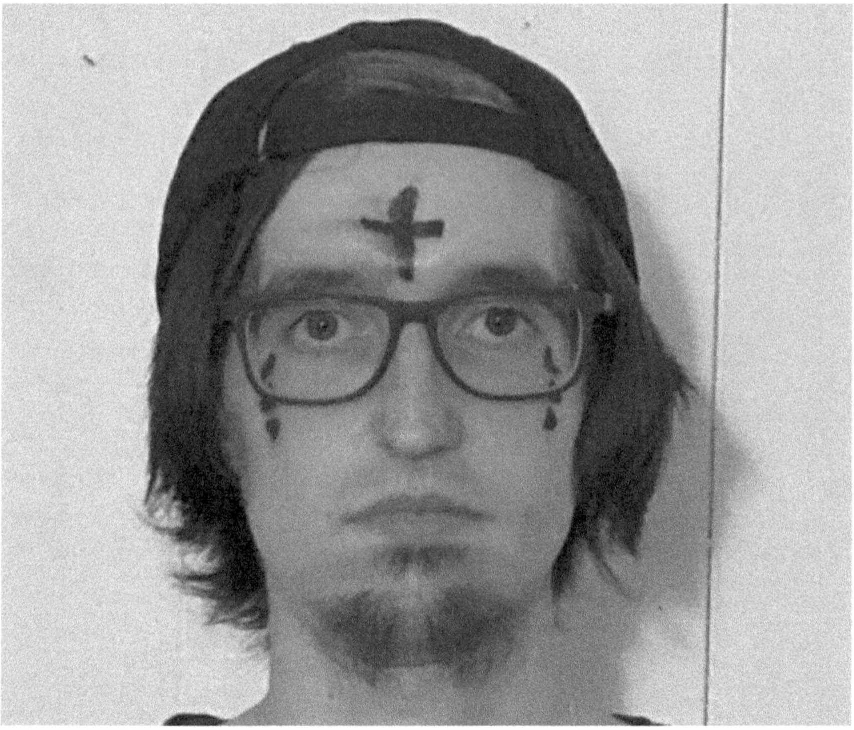

CPSIA information can be obtained
at www.ICGtesting.com
Printed in the USA
LVHW091928010621
688967LV00007B/3

9 781637 283332